Yes, Please

Other Titles by Willow Summers

Jessica Brodie Diaries

Back in the Saddle, Book 1
Hanging On, Book 2
A Wild Ride, Book 3

Growing Pains Series

Lost and Found, Book 1
Overcoming Fear, Book 2
Butterflies in Honey, Book 3
Growing Pains Boxed Set (books 1–3)
Love and Chaos, Cassie's Story

Surviving Love, a novel

Yes, Please

BY WILLOW SUMMERS

Chapter 1

———— ∞ ————

I DODGED A tourist on the busy sidewalk in downtown San Francisco. After stepping around another, I pushed through the glass door into the café before someone could bulldoze into me. The chill of the October day turned into lovely warmth as I did a quick sweep with my gaze. I noticed my friend immediately, sitting at the counter in the back with a book and a cup of coffee. It was hard to miss her. She had a shock of perfectly coiffured red hair falling in a loose curl to her mid-back. Her stylish clothes fit her body perfectly, accentuating her trim waist and natural curve. The latest in fashion, the knee-high boot on her left leg bounced slightly where it was gracefully draped over her right knee.

I threaded through the bustling space, dodging a chair that unexpectedly jutted toward me as someone tried to get up. "Oh, sorry!" I said as I turned sideways to squeeze by.

Kimberly looked up at the sound of my voice. She

greeted me with a flawless smile and moved her Louis Vuitton handbag off the chair beside her.

I'd met Kimberly during my freshman year in college. She had been a senior at the time and in the university's program to get promising freshmen on the right track. Most freshmen met their assigned senior once or twice, and then continued on with their lives. I would've done the same, not wanting to bother her, but week after week she'd checked in. As the year passed by, she was always there, supporting me and giving advice. And she still was. Nothing changed when she graduated. We weren't in the same social class and came from different backgrounds, but still she called me every week. She was sweet as well as beautiful, and I was thankful for her friendship.

I pulled out the high seat and hoisted myself up into it. "Hi," I said, laying the newspaper I was carrying on the counter and dropping my bag to the floor.

"Don't put it down there, it'll get dirty!" Kimberly started to bend for my bag.

I put my hand on her arm to stop her. "Kimberly, the thing is eight hundred years old, five shades lighter than when it was new, and probably dirtying the floor. It's fine."

She crinkled her nose at me but didn't argue. Instead, she glanced at the counter next to me. "Olivia, is that a *newspaper*?" Her incredulous gaze colored with humor. "Nineteen-eighty called—they want their communication device back."

I smiled as a server stopped by. The woman braced a pen to her green notepad. "Hi, what can I get for you?"

My mind went to the bills sitting on my bookshelf. If the stack were any taller, Godzilla would try climbing it. "Just a coffee, please."

"Do you want something to eat?" Kimberly asked me.

"Nah. I'm not hungry." To punctuate my lie, my stomach rumbled.

Kimberly looked at the server. "A turkey sandwich, no pickles, with a side of potato chips."

"You got it," the woman said as she scribbled down the order and moved away.

"When did you start eating meat?" I drummed my fingers on the counter to offset the sound of my stomach trying to tattle on me again.

She dropped the menu behind a napkin dispenser, where it flopped against the salt and pepper shakers. "I don't. But you're hungry, and you hate asking for handouts. It'll come, you'll bitch, and then I'll get to treat you to lunch. Just call me mastermind."

"Kimmy," I whined, picking at the edge of the newspaper. I could feel the heat saturate my cheeks. Pale skin and easy embarrassment were a couple of life's really cruel jokes. "You don't need to buy me lunch!"

"Oh, posh!" She snatched her phone off the counter, checked the screen, found no one had called or texted in the thirty seconds since she'd probably checked it last, and dropped it back down to the counter. "I got lucky and graduated when there were still jobs. I figure my luck will run out soon, and I'll get laid off. By then, you should be working, and you better expect to buy me lunch. See? Just planning ahead. So…"

She reached around me and grabbed the newspaper. "What are you doing with a newspaper? Old school. Why not look at Craigslist like everyone else?"

I blew out a breath. "My computer died. Actually, not true—it comes on. I can hear it buzzing, but the screen stays black. The tech guy I know said it'd be about four hundred dollars to fix, and that I should just buy a new one. Which is a great idea—I'd love to have a new computer. I'd also love to have four hundred bucks."

Kimberly tsked. "I have a computer you could borrow—it's old but it works. Robby bought me a new Mac."

Robby was Kimberly's rich, handsome boyfriend who was about five seconds away from slapping a ring on her finger. She was a great catch, and he was smart enough to realize it.

"Thanks! That'd be great. The library is fun and all, but my bedroom doesn't have stinky people leaning against the back of my chair."

Kimberly grimaced and ruffled the newspaper open like a father in a 1950s sitcom. The smile dripped off her face as her brow crinkled. "Admin assistant?" She glanced up at me.

I shrugged as my coffee arrived. I immediately reached for the creamer.

"But you got a degree in computer science…" Kimberly looked down at the listing again. "Computer science pays well. This… The salary isn't listed, but it can't be much."

I dumped two packets of sugar into my coffee. My spoon clinked as it whirled around the cup. I took a sip. The scalding brew raked down my throat and set my esophagus on fire. I coughed and beat at my chest. It didn't help. Eyes watering, I braced the counter until the heat dwindled.

"You should blow on it," Kimberly said.

"Mastermind, indeed," I wheezed. After the burn died away, I said, "I've been job hunting for six months, Kimberly. I started applying a month before I graduated, remember? A solid six months, too. No slacking. Out of applying for hundreds of positions, I've only gotten a handful of interviews. Then I always hear the same thing—the school I went to is impressive, my list of achievements are even more so, but I have no practical experience. Then I never hear from them again."

A surge of hopelessness welled up inside of me. Soon I'd have to start applying to fast food chains just to get some money coming in. The problem with that was it wouldn't be enough to keep a roof over my head. Not in this city, not even in the surrounding areas. Moving was inevitable, but I needed money for that, too.

Life was sure kicking me in the lady balls.

"I'm just looking for anything that pays at the moment," I said before chancing another sip. "I even applied to be a dog walker—turns out, there are more dog walkers around here than dogs."

"What about your mom?"

I scoffed. "On a safari with someone else's husband. She's never been much into the mothering game."

I shook my head and traced the cup's handle. "If I could just get *something*—literally anything that paid decently—I could keep afloat until the economy improves."

The sandwich arrived. With a busy smile, the waitress lowered the plate in front of Kimberly. "Can I get you anything else?"

"No, thank you. We're good." Kimberly pushed the plate in front of me as the waitress moved way. "Eat. This place does the best sandwiches."

I gave Kimberly a grateful smile. "I don't deserve you."

She laughed and picked up her phone. "I know of something…" she said slowly, cutting into the fog of a truly delicious sandwich. She chewed her lip, hesitating. Leaning forward elegantly on the counter, she lowered her voice to a soft whisper. "You're single, right?"

"Huh?" I asked, chewing.

"You're single?"

I rolled my eyes. "Kimberly, I love you, but for the love of God, don't try to set me up anymore. Either the guys take one look at me and make an excuse to get out of the date, or they just use me and dump me when they get bored. No thanks."

She flushed. "Sorry. I really thought Jonathan would've been a good match."

I waved it away, ignoring the little twinge in my gut from the handsome man who had taken my heart on the third date. He'd been charming and affectionate, and I was so blindly in love that when he broke it off, I laughed. I'd thought he was joking. He wasn't. Apparently I didn't fit in his world. He'd said, "You'd do better with someone more…your level."

"My level?" I'd screeched. "My level of awesome, you mean? Because yeah, I would!" And then I'd just started yelling nonsense and crying. It wasn't my finest moment.

"No big deal," I said to Kimberly. "Par for the course in my love life."

Kimberly gave me a beautiful pout before ducking her head. "Well…I do know of something—work related. It's kind of hush-hush, but…" She smiled in a dreamy way, and then flushed. "Hunter Carlisle is looking for a new assistant!"

"Hunter Carlisle?"

Her jaw dropped. "What rock have you been hiding under? He's the CEO of Primner and Locke! The youngest CEO they've ever had. And incredibly gorgeous." She paused and leveled me with a stare. "Incredibly."

The reference dawned as I sipped my coffee. From the little I'd heard, he was in his late twenties but had the business sense of someone far more experienced. He was shrewd and serious and in charge of a giant company with an equally large payroll. Getting my foot in there, in any capacity, would be a godsend.

A grin hijacked my confused expression. "I'm listening."

"So…I can get you an interview. He looks for intelligent women with raw talent, so your lack of experience won't be a problem as long as you tell him why you're looking for admin work when you are obviously way overqualified."

My heart sank, dwindling my smile. "Yes, but then he'll tell me that I'll get bored since I am overqualified. Either that, or he'll suspect that I'll try to transfer as soon as I can. I've been down this road before."

She shook her head adamantly. "No. He won't. He challenges his admins. He delegates work. He's really smart. I bet you'd learn a lot from him."

"Sounds too good to be true…"

"Well…" She hesitated. "There's a catch. He…um. Well, he kind of has a…strange contract. He requires long hours. As in…like, really long."

I shrugged and bit into my sandwich. Kimberly stared at me until I swallowed and finally said, "I don't mind long hours. For experience and a paycheck, I'll do just about anything."

Her stare intensified. "Well, that's just the thing. See, his life is the business, right? He's got a fiancée, but that's an arrangement to keep his family happy. He's not into her, and she doesn't bother with him. They don't get it on."

"I don't know what getting it on has to do with anything, but it doesn't matter. I don't care about long hours. I have no life."

Kimberly rolled her eyes. "Well, he's always working, and he's not into her, so he kind of has it set up where his admin fulfills all roles, you know?"

"What do you mean, all roles?"

"He...sorta...has his admin do work stuff, right? But then, when the mood strikes, she's like the girlfriend, too..."

I frowned as my brain slowly made sense of her words. I paused halfway to biting my sandwich when the full meaning hit me. Shivers worked up my body. "She does sexual stuff for him?" I whispered incredulously.

Kimberly flushed again, but this time, it was teamed with a light sheen of sweat. I realized something that made my heart beat faster and a strange tingle work through my core. She was aroused! The prospect of being an admin for a guy like Hunter Carlisle had her pupils dilating and her nostrils flaring. She was even breathing faster, as though she'd just finished running a mile. Or having sex.

I leaned in, suddenly feeling like two naughty schoolgirls in detention. "Why don't you apply?"

A sly smile crept up her face. She glanced around before lowering her voice to match mine. "I did. Last time he was looking. I got to the second round, but he chose someone else."

"Are you serious? You're not that kinda girl!"

She giggled, hiding her face in her hands. "I know! But the pay—" She dropped her hands and leaned back, rolling her eyes in delight. "The *man.*" She inhaled and fanned her face. "I had just that one time with him in the second interview. Oh my God, the way he—"

"Wait." I held my hand up to stop the words. Strange quivers filled my body. "Are you telling me he tries people out? Like…has sex with them?"

"Yes, and it was the absolute best sex of my entire life. I am not kidding. Women try to get interviews just for some time with him. But he is exclusive. He chooses his admin with care, and generally doesn't stray from her. Monogamous." Kimberly's voice dropped lower. She was fanning herself freely now. "It was so hot, Olivia. So, so hot. He was totally in control, and I swear it was just one big, long orgasm. Oh holy moly…"

She reached across me to grab my napkin and then dabbed her face.

"So…" My mind raced, not really believing my ears, and definitely not believing that Miss Goodie-Goodie Kimberly, who had never done anything crazy in college, was capable of something like this. Of doing something like this. And then passing it on to a friend!

I wanted to giggle, or squeal. My reaction to this revelation was as strange as the information itself. "How can that be legal?"

"Each person goes through a serious vetting process, with background checks and…other tests, and you get this lengthy contract going over all the working conditions just to be an admin. His office obviously has very sensitive information. And then there is this other contract for the more...personal side. And that protects him, lays out various stipulations, etc. You can say no at any time, but if you say no too often, he views it as a breach of contract. He needs the whole package."

"Do many girls say no?"

"*No!* Are you kidding? Just one time with him, and I'm addicted. I wouldn't say no."

"Then why does anyone leave?"

"For the same reason I'm not interviewing again—I have a steady boyfriend whom I love. Whom I might marry. I couldn't do that to him."

All I could do was blink. This should've been so far out of my comfort level that I shut the idea down immediately. This should've been so far out of Kimberly's! But something strange had taken over my body. Some wild streak that was tired of being stepped on. That was tired of being dragged through love only to realize I was being used. For once, I almost wanted to do something where the boundaries were clearly set, where there was no emotion, and both parties got what they wanted. Business. Blessed, unfeeling business.

"I cannot believe I am actually entertaining this," I said into my coffee.

"I know." Kimberly turned back to her nearly empty cup and stared down into its depths. "I couldn't believe I'd considered it, either. And then I couldn't believe I...you know. And here I am, totally wishing I could go for that interview. It's crazy. The whole setup is absolutely crazy, and you would not believe the high-powered professionals interviewing for it."

"And no one reports him?"

Kimberly waved her hand through the air, unconcerned. "The interviews are by invitation only. People know what they're getting into when they show up."

"And the other applicants…they're high-powered?"

"Oh yeah." Kimberly huffed. "And beautiful. I don't usually feel insecure, but…"

My mouth dried up. I had to swallow a few times just to croak out, "Why did you tell me? If you were insecure, I'll be the ugly girl in the corner."

Kimberly gave her customary sweet smile. "You will not! And why not you? You're really smart, really driven, and you have a bright future. I would've mentioned it sooner—even though it *is* a little…risqué—but I didn't know you'd be interested in admin work."

I gawked at her. "You thought I'd be fine with the…extra stuff, but didn't think the *work* was up my alley?"

Kimberly giggled. "It sounds ridiculous when you spell it out, but…yes. Totally." She giggled again. "Anyway, you're young, you have nothing going on, and you need the money—you owe it to yourself to meet him. That's probably all it'll take. And besides, I hear he treats his admins really well. No one has ever complained about any part of the job…"

I took another bite of my sandwich with butterflies

in my belly and confusion racing through my mind. I shook my head.

"I'll just text you the info…" Kimberly snatched her phone off the counter.

"Better write it down on the newspaper—my phone was cut off about an hour ago…"

LATER THAT NIGHT I walked into the apartment I shared with a roommate with Kimberly's laptop under my arm. She'd said it was her old one. It was at least two years newer than mine.

Her note with a date, time, address, and contact name of the interview with Hunter Carlisle burned in my pocket. I'd be crazy to go. Getting hired for admin work was one thing, but answering to a boss sexually as well?

Despite the insane tingles that blasted through me every time I thought about it, I just wasn't the type of girl that said yes to things like that. And if I was honest with myself—really, truly honest—I was confident with my shortcomings. I was a bit too curvy, a little too plain, and my overall vibe definitely too average. If Hunter Carlisle didn't hire a girl like Kimberly, there was no way I would even get in the door. I was okay with all that. The world needed plain, smart girls, too. I wasn't in a hurry to break my natural levelheadedness just to be turned down. Leave the fast lane for those seeking a thrill.

I dropped my stuff in my small bedroom and made

my way to the kitchen to make some tea. I wanted to look at the latest job postings before bed.

"Oh. You're home."

I winced as Jane, my roommate, slouched into the kitchen in holey sweats with stains down the front. Half of her hair had escaped her ponytail and now frizzed around her head. She leaned against the counter with a scowl.

"Rent is due in five days," she said in a dry voice.

I filled the kettle with water and switched it on. "I know, Jane. I'll have it."

"Well, you better, because I have someone interested in your room. No more late rent. You're late, and you get a notice. End of story."

Panic welled in my chest as I thought of my empty bank account. I had enough for one more month of rent. Just one.

"I'll have it," I said with a tight throat, feeling prickles in the back of my eyes. As Jane moved away with a huff, tears welled up. One overflowed and ran down my cheek, immediately leading to more. My situation was desperate. Graduating from a prestigious college was supposed to give a person a leg up, but all I got was a bunch of debt and shoved into the poor house.

I slunk back into my room with my cup of tea and drowning in tears. I set my cup down and fell into my bed. My blurry gaze drifted to the stack of bills that wouldn't be paid this month. Then down to my pocket where that strip of newspaper with Kimberly's writing burned against my hip.

Chapter 2

I CAN'T BELIEVE *I'm doing this.*

Five days after meeting Kimberly, I stood on the sidewalk downtown, looking up at a building reaching for the sky. Wide, tinted glass doors stood in front of me, stately and foreboding. A man exited the building, dressed in a crisp business suit. His gold cufflinks caught and threw the sun.

I didn't belong here.

I smoothed my slightly faded pinstripe skirt over my thighs. The black had turned a murky gray after too many washes. My pink blouse hung off my breasts in a shapeless avalanche. I'd changed my handbag to one of my better ones, but it definitely wasn't designer. And here I was, interviewing to be the assistant to the CEO.

I definitely did not belong here.

Summoning my courage, I strode forward. Belonging or not, questionable job description or not, I was broke and this was my only hope. Literally. I had actually been turned down from two fast food chains. I'd been informed they weren't hiring for managers and I was overqualified for the lower-level positions.

It was either this, or begging on the street.

This paid better.

Sucking in a deep breath, I entered the large lobby with a tight hold on my handbag. Marble and elegance stretched to either side, but I stayed focused on the man in uniform behind the large desk to the left. As I approached him, he looked up and lifted his brow. "Can I help you?"

"I'm here to see Mr. Carlisle. I have an appointment." I cleared my throat, hoping the action would scare away the tremor. It was a long shot, granted.

The man touched his computer monitor. After scanning the screen for a moment, he said, "Just go ahead and sign in here, if you would."

He touched the monitor facing me at the end of the counter.

"Oh, sure." I shook out my hands. It was also ineffective in chasing away the tremor.

The keyboard was right below the monitor, and I quickly filled in the needed information. The man consulted his own screen before hitting a few buttons and printing out a badge. He handed it over then pointed toward the back of the lobby. "Just take elevator thirteen all the way up to level fifty-three."

I smiled and thanked him as I moved woodenly to the elevators. I exited at the appropriate floor and saw three women waiting in leather chairs. Opposite them were three more chairs, with a shiny coffee table sitting between them. To the left, an older women with half-moon reading glasses stared at a computer monitor at the side of her desk. Next to her, an identical desk stood currently bare.

I approached her slowly, fist squeezing the handle of my bag. I wanted to exude confidence, but with nervousness eating away at my insides, I was more concerned about not getting sick.

She gazed at me over the rim of her glasses.

"Hi," I croaked. I cleared my throat and tried again. "Hi. I'm here to apply? For the position?"

"Your name, please." The woman's expression remained bland, unperturbed by my faulty start.

"Olivia Jonston."

She glanced at her computer, clicked the mouse a few times, and nodded. "Please have a seat until I call your name."

I nodded and started over, knowing my face was glistening with nervous perspiration. I rounded one of the empty chairs and sat slowly, getting a good look at my competition. Then I had the urge to laugh hysterically.

The three women in front of me were drop-dead gorgeous. Absolutely beautiful. Blond hair, one and all, was either done up perfectly with no flyaways, or hanging in a loose tumble over slim shoulders. Their clothes were professional and pristine, suits tailored to fit dynamite bodies. Pearls or gold necklaces adorned thin necks, and flawless makeup enhanced jaw-dropping faces.

I needed more makeup than any of these, and I was wearing the least. *Just call me Underdog.*

"Ginger Stevens," the woman behind the desk called.

Beauty number one bent to the side and picked up a designer handbag of some sort—I vaguely recognized the symbol from a red carpet picture. With the other hand, she picked up a leather folder and gracefully rose from her seat.

With horror I realized everyone had folders, leather-bound and expensive. These women were bringing portfolios rather than their meager résumés.

I glanced down at the piece of paper resting in my lap. I didn't even have enough experience to take up two sheets, let alone fill a portfolio.

Seriously, what was I doing here?

I inched up my chin. Getting down on myself wouldn't help. I wasn't pretty, fine, but I had great work ethic. I also had a reputable school under my belt. And I'd done a bunch of activities in school that taught me leadership and organization and…other important things.

I rummaged around in my brain for more great qualities as the next woman was called. She elegantly brushed a loose curl over her shoulder as she rose.

My gaze slid down her shapely legs and stuck to her fabulous red heels. I noticed the same emblem on those as she had on her handbag.

So…designer, then. Her suit surely was, too. She was

wearing money. It was probably stitched into her seams and stuffed in her pockets.

I shook my head a fraction and looked away at the window, calling up my selling points and things I might say. I'd been through an interview or two; I had experience with most of the questions. Not that it had helped in the past, but maybe this time would be different.

You said that last time.

I curled my fists in exasperation at myself as the next woman was called. Not able to help it, I thought about who else might be hiring. Fast food was out, but what about Starbucks? I heard they were a cool company—I could give them a try.

Was there a Target nearby?

It took me a moment to recognize my name hovering in the air.

It dawned on me that the third woman had disappeared. I'd been completely lost in my own world.

I peeked my head around the chair back. The woman at the desk was staring at me over her half-moon glasses, waiting for me to get in gear.

I popped up and straightened my clothes before grabbing my handbag. I smiled at the woman as I approached, hoping the sentiment reached my eyes.

"Go on in," she said, not smiling back.

I passed her desk and turned toward the partially open door. Taking a deep breath, I laid my hand on the cool handle and gently pushed. The large room spread out before me. Huge windows filled the wall at the far end of the room, showing the clear blue sky beyond. A round table surrounded by four chairs crouched off to my left. A couch lay ten feet beyond that, with a coffee table in front of it, and two large chairs to the other side. And in front of me, only slightly removed to the side, was a giant desk with two chairs in front.

A man stood as I entered. My jaw went slack and my mouth fell open. Like that first plunge on a roller coaster, my stomach flipped, and then dropped with the free fall.

Kimberly had mentioned Hunter Carlisle was attractive. Incredibly gorgeous, she had said.

She had grossly understated his appearance.

He had a strong jaw, high cheekbones, and straight nose. A top-dollar tailored suit swathed the muscular vee of his torso, leading down to trim hips and solid thighs. His delicious bedroom eyes, hooded as though in the throes of ecstasy, were a deep, bottomless brown, entrancing. Confidence and charisma oozed from his powerful body, melting my bones. His masculinity did not ask me to yield, but demanded it.

On shaking legs threatening to buckle, I walked closer with a lump in my throat. I didn't dare speak. It would only come out in a warbled mess.

"Olivia?" he asked, his keen gaze rooting me to the floor.

I struggled to take a breath.

"Olivia Jonston, correct?" he asked.

"Yes," I whispered, something hot and fiery settling deep into my core.

"Take a seat." He moved around his desk with the grace of a dancer and stood behind one of the large chairs, as though pulling it out for me.

Walking like the Tin Man with rusty hinges, I crossed the distance and took the proffered seat, getting a whiff of his aftershave. I closed my eyes, savoring the mouthwatering elixir. Unbidden, wetness blossomed between my thighs.

Suddenly I knew *exactly* what Kimberly had been talking about; exactly why she'd flushed every time she mentioned his name. I knew why gorgeous, high-powered women lined up for a job probably way under their pay grade and professional level.

It was to be close to Hunter Carlisle.

I glanced up into those sexy, smoldering eyes, and just stared. I didn't know what came next, but I was pretty sure I needed a moment to get ready for it.

"Did you bring your résumé?" Mr. Carlisle asked.

"Y-yes, of course," I stammered, picking it off the ground where it had fluttered after my fingers lost their grip. The sheet trembled as I handed it across the desk.

He stared at me quietly for a moment before his gaze dipped to the page. He dropped the page to his desktop and resumed his scrutiny of me.

"Tell me," he started in a deep voice that vibrated down my spine and tickled parts of me that were distinctly feminine. "Why would a Stanford grad in a sought-after field turn up in my office applying for an admin role?"

I willed saliva into my mouth to cure the sudden dryness. "As you see"—I pointed a shaky finger at his desktop where my résumé lay—"I graduated five months ago. I've been diligently searching for work, but at the moment, there aren't opportunities for those without experience, however great the school I graduated from."

The words sounded professional, but my tone was much too wispy. The sheen of sweat on my face screamed *uncomfortable*. Or, more correctly, *turned on*. I was out of control without a clue how to fix matters.

His gaze traveled my face, and then grazed my body. When he was once again looking into my eyes, he said, "The economy is lagging at present. You're unlucky in your timing."

"I've come to that realization," I heard myself say. The words were like an echo from someone else. Wobbly and distorted. I was not in charge of my linguistics. I only hoped he attributed it to nervousness.

"Olivia?"

"What was that?" I blurted.

Humor sparked in his eyes. "I said, would you be open to tasks outside of that strictly administrative? I have a variety of projects that come through this office, or that need overseeing."

"Yes, of course."

"And hours? Do you have a preference?"

A blush crept up my face as heat saturated my body. "No. I'm always available," I said in a breathy voice I did not recognize. *Get a grip!*

He leaned forward, bracing his elbows on his desk. "Tell me about your hobbies. Your usual day."

Caught off guard with a non-interview question, and with my mind on complete hiatus in his company, I just blurted out what came to mind. Unfortunately, that turned out to be the minute details of my life. I told him everything, from my morning walk, to getting inventive with what was in the fridge. When he asked about my job search, I stupidly told all, one rejection to the next. I didn't add flourishes or hold anything back. All my faults I laid bare, and all the things I excelled at I bluntly offered up. I just opened my mouth and purged.

He sat and watched me, gaining all my life's secrets with a focused, almost predatory gaze. Only when shadows started crawling across the floor from the neighboring high rises did the question and answer segment slow, and finally stop. Silence descended as he sat and stared at me. My heart thumped under that handsome gaze.

The swish of expensive fabric was the only sound as he rose. "I think that'll be all for today. Check in with my assistant on your way out. You'll hear from my office either way."

"Oh." I painfully uncrossed my right leg from my left before I stood. My skin peeled away, leaving a red mark. *Ouch.*

I stood, a little lopsided, and tried to get my bearings. I should've switched positions at least once during the interview to prevent my leg from falling asleep.

After shaking it out, aware that I was the subject of scrutiny, I stepped forward to leave. My numb leg gave out. My knee knocked into the back of the desk with a loud *thud*. I fell forward, ungracefully sprawling across his desktop.

In a panic, I tried to right myself, but my leg was mostly useless. It stayed limp as my left leg pushed upward. My body swung toward the right.

I grunted, scrabbling my fingers across his desk, trying to find purchase and stop the slide. My elbow smashed into his phone, knocking it to the floor. Pens became airborne, launching across the desk. I grabbed the edge of his desk pad, dragging it with me as I tipped over the side. Gravity pulled at me greedily. My face rushed toward the ground.

Before I hit, strong hands grabbed me around the middle and hoisted me up. The desk pad crashed down. My résumé fluttered after it.

I knew a moment of confusion before I was righted, my body pulled into a chest so hard it could've been stone, flexed from picking me up in a dead weight. I clutched his shoulders, feeling the bulge of muscle through his suit jacket.

A sigh escaped my mouth. My lady parts tightened and then swelled, aching with the proximity of a man this divine. I melted against his body.

"Are you okay?" That deep bass tickled me in exquisite ways.

"Sorry." The word floated on another sigh before

reality smashed into my consciousness.

I was draping myself on the CEO of a huge, world-wide company. In an interview!

"Oh my God," I said, panicking again. "I am so sorry!"

I struggled out of his grasp. Pins and needles accosted my leg. Each movement vibrated up my bones painfully, but I ignored it. I reached down for my handbag. My leg wobbled, making me stagger into the chair. Righting myself, I brushed the hair from my face before avoiding his outstretched hands, like a star quarterback with the ball. I hobbled out into the open space, humiliation at my loss of control spurring me on. "I'm so sorry about that! Really!"

I said the last over my shoulder as I limped out of the door and shut it behind me. In a daze of mortification, I used the empty desk as support to get over to the older assistant. She'd been looking at me already, so I just threw it out there: "I'm supposed to check in with you?"

Her eyebrows pinched together as humor danced in her eyes. She glanced down at my hands gripping the desk. "Are you okay?"

"Oh. Yeah. My leg fell asleep. I kind of stumbled out of there." A grin tickled her lips, so I finished up with, "It was embarrassing."

The grin widened into a smile. "At least you'll be hard to forget." She held up a piece of paper. I limped over, trying to shake my leg out as I reached her desk. "Please make sure I have the correct contact info." She tapped the paper after she laid it near my hands at the edge of her desk.

As I studied the page, she continued, "Haven't interviewed in a while, I take it?"

"Oh." I wiped my forehead of moisture as I straightened up. "I have, actually. A lot. But not for a CEO. Or, you know, someone that…intense."

"Ah." The woman continued to survey me. I had a feeling there was a joke hovering in the air, and the fact that I wasn't in on it meant I was probably the punch line.

Time to go.

I pointed at my number on the piece of paper. "That's correct, but, unfortunately, it isn't turned on at the moment. Email would be the best way to reach me. Or Skype. I have Wi-Fi in the apartment."

"Yes, of course." She turned to her monitor. Her fingers flew over her keyboard, making a note. "We'll let you know within three business days."

"Oh, great. Thanks," I mumbled. I gave her a departing smile and walked from the area, my limp now decidedly less noticeable. It wasn't until I was walking through the building's lobby that I realized I hadn't even offered to help clean up Mr. Carlisle's desk. I'd spilled half the contents to the ground, and then run from the room.

I closed my eyes and moaned at my stupidity. It was, quite possibly, the worst interview I'd ever had. I'd gone on a tirade about my situation and my constant rejections from other employers, something a person should *never* do with a prospective boss, and then told him about the stupid details of my daily life—I even told him about my money problems! That was something I hadn't told anyone.

"What is *wrong* with me?" I mumbled, having a passerby glance at me in confusion.

It was safe to say that even if I had been on an even playing field with the other candidates, I was not getting a red carpet to that position.

I immediately went in search of a Starbucks.

Chapter 3

M Y PHONE RANG.
In confusion, I glanced over to where it lay at the edge of my bed.

It rang again.

I pushed the computer out of my way and leaned over, seeing "Blocked" on the screen.

It rang a third time.

I hadn't paid my bill. So why was my phone ringing?

I picked it up and swiped the screen. Putting it to my ear like it might explode, I gave a hesitant, "Hello?"

"Miss Olivia Jonston?" came a woman's voice.

"Yes?"

"This is Brenda Jones of Mr. Carlisle's office…"

It had been two days since the interview and I'd tried to clear the whole scene from my head. His face had swum up periodically, as had the feel of his hard body against mine, but other than that, it was a life lesson in how *not* to interview.

I knew I would be getting this call, though—

rejection number eight hundred billion and eleven.

"Yes, hello," I said pleasantly, wanting to get this over with. Closure was always good, after all. It helped a person progress to better things.

At least, that was what I had been telling myself these last two days.

"Hi," Brenda said. "I wanted to inform you that Mr. Carlisle would like to invite you to a follow-up interview in four days."

It felt like champagne bubbles worked up the center of my body. A ringing sounded in my head.

"I have just emailed you the particulars," she continued. "Please read over the materials and get back to me with any questions. Congratulations and good luck."

I barely got out a "thanks" before the emptiness of a disconnected line descended. I pulled the phone away from my head and stared at it dumbly.

I got a follow-up interview? How did I get a follow-up interview?

"And why is my phone activated?" I said.

My gaze shifted to my computer. A number one in a red oval hovered over my mailbox icon. With shaking hands I clicked on it. The email from Brenda Jones popped up with a list of expectations. I was to report to a different office in the building to take some software tests, which would probably be various Microsoft Office products. When finished, I was to report to Mr. Carlisle's office with my signed contracts in hand for the follow-up interview. She judged it would take two hours from start to finish.

Butterflies raging through my ribcage, I opened the attachments. The first was a standard contract of employment, binding the signer to remain silent with the sensitive materials when in the company's employ. The contract seemed general, in that it was for anyone entering employment within the company.

Hardly breathing, I opened the other contract. This was shorter, and infinitely more personal. Mr. Carlisle was named here specifically. In addition, my name appeared instead of "employee." My "uniform," such as it was, was a skirt and a blouse, or a dress. No slacks, unless specifically requested. High heels and tights or nylons were optional unless specifically requested. Makeup was optional as well. Again, unless specifically requested.

> * Miss Olivia Jonston shall have the right to say "no" or "stop" at any time, and in any situation. She is never to be harmed, bound, muffled, gagged, or given to another, unless expressly desired. In that situation, an amendment must be signed.

> * It is mutually agreed that if Miss Olivia Jonston uses her freedom of will to deny Mr. Hunter Carlisle more than five times per month, or for more than three times per month for three consecutive months, possible termination will result.

> * Mr. Carlisle may request attendance with Miss Olivia Jonston at any time during work hours, or during a work function, and in any location. However, visibility of nudity by others will be minimized at all times.

The list went on. It was clear Mr. Carlisle had his admin's comfort in mind within this setup, making sure she was at ease and looked after, but it was equally clear that he was in charge. He called the shots: he said when, how and how much, and he controlled each situation.

Shivers racked my body. I'd never completely given in to anyone. I'd come close with Jonathan, but there was always that element of myself that I'd held back. That I protected. I'd always maintained that little bit of control over my desires, my situation, and my body.

Hunter Carlisle was asking me to give that up.

No, not that I give it up, but that I give it to him.

Fighting the fear and strange shivers, I quickly tapped Kimberly's name in my phone. It was answered on the second ring. "Oh my God, I've been trying to get hold of you!"

"Hi." I settled back on my bed, away from the contract pulled up on my screen.

"Did you go?" Kimberly asked in a hush.

"Yes," I said.

Kimberly squealed, a distinctly preteen sound. "I *knew* you would. Although, to be honest, I half thought you wouldn't, too. If anyone could deny him, it would be you. But I definitely thought you going was a possibility."

"I got a call back—I'm staring at the personal contract right now."

"Oh my God," she said again, the words low and drawn out. "I *knew* he'd see your potential! I talked to a friend of mine, and Mr. Carlisle interviewed about thirty people over a few days. He only chose *three* people to bring back. Usually he chooses five." She squealed. "Sorry," she said, out of breath. "I feel like I'm twenty-two again."

I didn't mention that she wasn't much older than that now. "Okay, but the personal contract…"

"What about it?" she asked, calming down.

"I mean…he's totally in charge. It's a bit…daunting."

"The man is *always* in charge. He rules any room he's in. And trust me, you want him in that role." She sighed into the phone. "He's good at it."

I stared at the computer screen in uncertainty. I didn't know if I could give someone else complete control over my body, regardless of his ability to take the lead. It was a lot of liberty to hand over to a complete stranger. Especially a man, and *especially* when that man was thinking strictly with his anatomy.

"I don't know," I whined, closing the laptop. "I need the job, but I'm just… This just isn't *me,* you know?"

"Trust me, it isn't any of us. Not strictly speaking, anyway. You think a bunch of high-powered, smart, educated women would give up their careers to be an assistant? No way. The business experience his admins get is priceless. He's a great employer, he pays well, and his name opens doors. Yes, there is this little issue of…naughtiness, we'll say, but trust me, the way he treats the situation is so calm and run of the mill, and the way he just…*is*. Is he a man you want to say no to? Even in a personal situation?"

I thought back to his commanding presence; to his aura of power and dominance; to his appearance and body. Fire licked at my core.

No, he wasn't a man I would walk away from. That was part of the problem. I didn't trust that I could stick to my guns with him. I feared I would lose myself to his desires and demands, and with it, lose all the confidence I'd worked so hard to gain.

"I don't know…"

"It's your choice. Think about it. My advice? Meet him again. See what he's about on the personal side of things. If you aren't interested, you aren't interested. No big deal. In the meantime, Daddy has an opening in the IT department. It's still beneath your education level, but it's a start."

A huge surge of hope filled me. Gratitude welled up next. "You begged him, didn't you?"

The line was silent for a moment before she said, "*Well?* Your talent is just going to waste with no job. You'd be a valuable asset."

Kimberly had seen me at my wits' end and tried to help. She was the best sort of person. "I should say no."

"You can't say no!" She laughed. "I had to beg him. I told him you might have something else, so I gave you the *out,* just in case. But he's a good fallback. The boss of the department is a bit stupid, but he works hard and he's fair."

"Sounds like a dream," I said through my smile. "I owe you one. I owe you a million, what am I saying?" Tears of gratitude came to my eyes. Suddenly, the situation with Hunter Carlisle wasn't as big a deal. I had a fallback. A legitimate fallback that would at least pay me enough to keep me afloat, if I knew Kimberly.

She laughed into the phone. "You are my project, and I will not rest until everyone sees how beautiful and intelligent you are!"

"I don't even care that I'm your charity case," I said with glee.

"Okay, stop by my place tomorrow and we'll set you up with some clothes for both interviews. Because those are the terms—I will only help you if you promise to at least hear Mr. Carlisle out. He would be insanely good for both your career and sex drive. If anything, he'll help you get back on the horse and stop dwelling on that jerk Jonathan!"

I just smiled. I didn't know how, but some day, I would repay her!

FOUR DAYS LATER I entered the huge building down-town in a suit and heels. True to form, Kimberly had set me up with the best her closet had to offer. Even if the outfit was a bit snug in places, and the heels insanely hard to walk in for someone with very little practice, it still looked much better than anything I had.

I'd interviewed with her father's company the day before, a mid-level organization that did pretty well for itself. The boss seemed to like me, and the green light had already been given, so he'd extended me an offer right there. I would've taken it right there, too, so desperate for a steady income I was salivating over it, but I had promised Kimberly. Plus, the offer was for a minuscule salary that would barely cover all my bills. I could survive on it, but it would be a lean couple of years.

I reported to the front desk as before, and signed in. Instead of the top floor, this time I was directed to the thirty-second floor. Once there, I checked in with a clerk and was immediately led into a small room where I was given four tests to complete—three Microsoft Office products and a proofreading test. The proofreading was by far the hardest for me, being from a computers background and heavily using code and spell-check.

When I'd finished, I stuck my head outside the room and caught the clerk's attention. She glanced up. "Did you have a question?"

"No, I'm finished," I answered.

With a startled expression, she glanced at the clock on her desk. "Already? You did all three?"

I nodded. "Yes, all three."

"My goodness." She smiled as she took my proof-reading sheet. "Great. You're all set. Report to your hiring manager."

"Thanks," I said, trying to ignore the butterflies filling my stomach at the prospect of seeing Mr. Carlisle again.

I took the elevator and once again appeared in front of Brenda, but this time, there was no one else waiting.

"Have a seat. He'll be with you in a moment," Brenda said as she glanced up.

My breathing became labored and my stomach started to roll again. I'd be confronted with those eyes. I'd see that body, so tall and hard, imagining that it was cut with muscle and defined within an inch of perfection.

I shivered as I clutched my borrowed leather binder, wiping those thoughts from my mind. I had an agenda here today. This was a possible business deal. I needed salary numbers, information on the benefit plan, possible hours I would be working, and other relevant information to the position. I would ignore his good looks and deep, sexy voice, and I would definitely ignore any sexual advances unless I was positive this job was better than my other offer.

I glanced at my phone, peeking out of my purse. My brow furrowed.

I will also ignore that the name on the credit card used to pay my phone bill was Hunter Carlisle.

That was just another controlling tactic, I was sure. I was in charge here.

I nodded with a firm expression, responding to my inner pep talk.

"Miss Jonston, he'll see you now," came Brenda's voice.

My stomach jumped into my throat, then plummeted as though I had just stepped off a cliff. I croaked out a barely intelligible response before moving on stiff legs into the battle room.

So much for that inner pep talk…

Bright light streamed in through the windows and flowed across the wide shoulders of Hunter Carlisle as he sat at his desk, watching me enter.

Clutching my binder just a little tighter, I took a seat in front of him. The *cush* of my leather chair broke the silence.

He leaned back, surveying me. "You're all business today. And you've come better prepared. Gearing up for battle?"

I gulped. In addition to being gorgeous and powerful, was he also a mind reader? Because that was exactly what I had been thinking…

"What's in the folder?" he prompted.

I opened the leather folder on my lap. On one side was my résumé with the contracts tucked behind, one signed, one not. On the other was a notepad with my scrawled questions. Having it typed would've looked nicer, but without a printer, there wasn't much I could do.

"I just have a few questions reserved for the end of the interview, if I may. Along with the various requested documentation," I answered professionally.

His gaze turned amused. "Is that so? Well, then, let's start the interview. You don't mind if I go first?"

"No. Please." I gave a stiff nod to match my tight voice, trying to remind myself that he wasn't in charge of me. Not yet, and probably not ever. Even if I was offered this job, over the other two, no doubt beautiful, women in the running, I would be hard-pressed to take it over my other, safer offer. This was a meeting of minds, nothing more.

"You've talked to Kimberly Feely about this position?" he began.

"Yes. She invited me to interview after having ascertained that I was looking for positions outside of my specific skill set."

His amused eyes began to sparkle. "Eloquent. And she filled you in on the various duties of this position, including those only spoken about in select circles?"

"Yes, sir," I replied, fighting the breathiness of my voice.

"And you've read and reviewed both contracts regarding this position?"

"Yes, sir." I patted my binder.

"Give them to me."

"Sure," I said softly as I pulled them out and handed them across the desk. My cheeks heated in embarrassment as the personal contract was exposed, lacking the signature required at the bottom of each page.

His gaze left me briefly to glance down at the documents lying on his desk, before returning to analyze me. He didn't reach for either packets of paper. Instead, he rolled to his computer and clicked his mouse a few times. A low hum sounded beneath him. He resumed his stare at me until the machine stopped, and then he reached down. He handed a sheet of paper across the desk.

With a furrowed brow, I took it, recognizing it as my test scores from a few minutes before.

"Impressive," he said, clasping his hands in his lap. "You've set a record in this office. Not even Brenda, who I employ solely for general administrative duties, has scored higher. One hundred percent on Excel and Word, ninety-nine on PowerPoint, and ninety-five on proof-reading. Your average typing speed is incredibly fast while still being accurate."

"That test wasn't really geared for advanced users..." I picked at the corner of the binder, knowing I should be affirming the scores in confidence, rather than being defensive about them. But his gaze had turned so piercing that I felt pinned down. I felt like the battle for control had begun, and I was already two breaths from losing.

"No. Even so, you have set a record I doubt will be broken for some time. I've spoken to some of your professors—they gave nothing but glowing reviews for you."

Surprise flitted through me, but I didn't speak. I didn't even know what I'd say if he'd asked me to speak. No other interviewer had ever called a teacher—at least, not that I knew of.

"Your roommate doesn't like you much," he continued. "But after speaking to her, that only works in your favor."

Surprise turned to shock. "You talked to my roommate?"

"Yes." He leaned forward, studying me again. "I tried to contact your mother as well. She was unavailable. I should note that I know her current...travel partner professionally. I have also met her travel partner's wife. Say the word, and that affair will be ended. I do not like sneaking behind the backs of people we have pledged our honesty and trust to."

I felt my face color in disbelief. When I applied for the job, I'd had no idea he would research me this thoroughly. I hadn't even given him this information—he had gone about hound-dogging me on his own. And now he was asking me to interfere in my mother's twisted relationship, something I hadn't done since her and my dad's divorce.

"I stay out of my mother's business," I managed, trying not to splutter.

He nodded as if he thought that was the case. "Then I'll deal with it as I deem necessary."

"Do you..." I cleared my throat to put a little strength in my voice. "Do you do such thorough research on all your interviewees?"

"Of those who advance to the next level, yes. This job is about two people working cohesively. I have no doubt you can do the day-to-day duties. All of the applicants could handle those. What I need to know is how you work under pressure, what your background is, your work ethic, things like that. I need to know the type of person I'm bringing with me into the trenches, so to speak.

"I'll also need to know that the person can operate on a personal level. My admin and I will be obligated to attend dinners, conferences, and other events. I need to know that my chosen partner can carry on conversations, can handle details, and can stay by my side for fifteen hours without each of us growing tired or angry with the other. This job is as much about personality as it is about ability. My admin and I form a tight bond for as long as she is in my employ, and I protect that bond with everything in my power."

Shivers traveled my body, turning into the heat I was starting to grow accustomed to. I nodded, still not knowing what to say.

After analyzing me for a moment, he continued, "You've had a series of shallow boyfriends, starting with your first love in your senior year of high school."

My jaw went slack. "How could you possibly know that?"

"He cheated on you, correct? And from there you dated similar types of men that all let you down one way or another, ending with Jonathan Banks."

My mouth snapped shut as pain consumed me. That breakup still hurt. *All* those breakups hurt, in one way or another. I'd been cheated on, lied to, ignored—I'd had a terrible track record with men. Something I didn't like to tell others, for fear of being pitied. I didn't want people to wonder what was wrong with me that I couldn't hold on to a guy.

And now, here I was, sitting in an interview for a job I didn't really want, getting grilled about these horrible love lessons. If Hunter Carlisle was trying to knock me off balance, he was doing a damned fine job.

"Why would any of this matter?" I asked, blinking away the sudden rise of emotion.

"I am counting on you being jaded with love."

What the hell did me being jaded with love have to do with...

And then I knew why. Before he even spoke again, I knew exactly what was coming next.

"I'm going to be frank, Miss Jonston," he said in a level tone. "Everything about this position hinges on the ability to remain emotionally detached. I'm not a hearts and flowers kind of guy. I'm an employer. My assistant and I will be physically intimate, but not emotionally so. To help maintain the boundary, I never kiss her lips, I don't hold her hand, or do anything else that might confuse the circumstances. I won't serenade you, Olivia, I'll fuck you. And you'll like it."

Fireworks went off in my body. I couldn't tell if the thrill was from fear or arousal.

I should've gotten up and walked out right then. I should've flipped him the bird and left. But the fire consuming me wouldn't let me move. Despite my reservations, of which there were plenty, I knew he was right. If he was even half as good as Kimberly said, I *would* like it. A lot. And that terrified me.

Breathing heavily, the pounding in my core matching the rush in my ears, I barely heard him continue. "You might be wondering what you'd get out of this situation?"

I didn't answer. I was trapped in his predatory gaze.

"I have excellent connections, Olivia, not to mention that this position would open the door to departmental transfer. My assistants aren't forever, and I wouldn't expect you to stay past the two years necessary to transfer. I have all kinds of work crossing my desk. I would challenge you. I'd give you an education in business to rival that of computer sciences. You'd be better prepared for the work force after our time together."

He leaned forward, placing his elbows on the desk. "I want you, Olivia. Don't think of this arrangement as a woman might traditionally think of sex—don't think with your heart. Marry the job, like I have. Get intimate with your business partner, take what you need from me—use me—and then move on. Glorious, unfeeling business. It is the cure-all in situations like yours. And has always been in situations like mine."

I stared into that commanding gaze. I didn't know what to say. How to act. He'd laid it all out for me, not bashful in the least. Not apologetic about what he was asking of me. In fact, he put the advantages in my hands, inviting me to use him. Suggesting I put myself into his employ with the understanding I would benefit the most from it.

"Why me?" I couldn't help but ask. "I don't have half of what those other women do. Look at me."

His gaze bored into mine, unflinching. "I am looking at you."

I smoothed out my skirt, turning away.

"I want you, Olivia," he said softly, standing. "You would be perfect in this role. I've met with the two other candidates, and they're not as smart as you, as driven, nor as malleable. I can shape you into excellence. You have the fundamentals, and I have the business experience. You could be great. In time you could lead a company like this one."

He came around the desk. Standing over me, his power shocked into my being. His command, and strength, his confidence, had my heart hammering as I looked up at that godlike face.

His eyes smoldered. "I want to fuck you, Olivia, whenever I want, however I want. And I want you to beg me for it." He took the binder out of my limp hands. "Stand up."

I stood before I knew what I was doing. He threw the binder to the side as those intense, lust-darkened eyes stared down into mine. He tilted my chin up and then bent, running his lips against the fevered skin of my neck.

"I want to make you scream my name," he murmured as his lips reached my jaw line. His hand dropped slowly, traveling down my chest and then over the swell of my breast.

"Tell me you want to fuck me." His voice was soft, but the command underneath was undeniable.

I moaned, words unintelligible as that firm hand worked down my stomach. It left my body, then returned to my inner thigh. I closed my eyes, feeling his soft lips gently sucking at my neck. My body leaned into him, wanting this. Wanting him like I'd never wanted anyone's touch in my life.

"Tell me you want to fuck me. That you want to become mine," he urged in that deceptively soft voice.

His hand slowly worked up my inner thigh. My body trembled under his touch. My sex swelled with a need I couldn't even begin to describe or understand. I couldn't think. I could barely stand.

"Say it, Olivia. Say you're mine."

His hand reached my apex and moved over my panty-covered sex. I knew he could feel my wetness through the material. I whimpered as he rubbed softly. His digits moved to the edge before dipping under the lace lining and touching me, skin on skin.

"Ohhh," I sighed, my core winding up. My breath coming in fast pants.

"Tell me, Olivia," he repeated. His words were nothing more than breath on my ear. His fingers traced along my slit before firmly pushing inside of me, angled just right.

"Oh God," I moaned, my eyes fluttering, my hands gripping his shoulders. "Please."

"Please what, Olivia?" he asked, moving two fingers in and out. He worked a thumb to the top, circling my nub with firm pressure.

"Oh please," I begged. I wanted to bring his face closer to mine for a deep, sensuous kiss. To explore his mouth as he explored my body.

His fingers sped up as dawning fought my desire-soaked thoughts. I recalled what he'd said about kissing. The words he had used, and was using. Fuck me. Make me his.

He wanted to consume me. To strip me out of my body and mold me in a way he thought best.

The pleasure climbed, but so did the fear. The fear of letting go. The fear of losing control. The fear of someone taking from me the only thing I could truly call my own—free will.

I pushed away, fighting my desire. Fighting my impulses. His hands fell away immediately. I staggered backward, not able to look up into his eyes. Afraid I'd give in totally if I did.

Instead, I reached down and snatched up my handbag. I turned and walked for the door with a shaky step. The other job might not pay well, but it was purely professional, rather than having strings attached. I just didn't trust myself with Hunter Carlisle. I didn't trust that once I started saying yes, I could ever again say no.

Chapter 4

⟿

TWO DAYS LATER, the cool air hit my face as I walked down the street. I glanced at the paltry trees spaced along the edge of the sidewalk, their leaves turning a rustic orange and yellow with the waning season, and recalled the fire in Hunter Carlisle's hooded eyes. Bedroom eyes. Sexy and intelligent, his gaze had stripped away my layers and rendered me a throbbing, pulsing mess.

It was two *long* days since I'd run out of his office like a scared fawn. Since the hottest man I'd ever met had tempted me with coarse words, and then made me go hazy with a deft hand.

I'd never experienced a man like him. The things he said should've made me want to slap him. Instead, I wanted to see him again. The effect he had on me made no sense. I wasn't a prude or anything, but "fuck me" and "tell me you're mine" weren't usually up my alley. Yet here I was, walking down the street, daydreaming about the feel of his hard chest under my palms. Or his soft lips grazing my skin. Or his voice, telling me to give in.

I shivered.

Maybe it was a good thing I'd fled like a vampire from sunlight. My poor attempt at professionalism and self-control ended with his fingers tracing my panty line. I was no match for someone like him. If I gave him control, it would end in my getting attached, and him ripping my heart out like all the others.

No dice.

I took a deep breath as I made my way to a café where Kimberly waited for me, desperate to hear all the details. I'd talked to her on the phone, but something about my high-pitched, frenzied account of the hours I'd lost to his office left her unsatisfied.

I wrestled my thoughts away from the dominating and confident man as I approached the few tables set up on the sidewalk of North Beach, an area known as the Italian District of San Francisco. Kimberly awaited me at a table closest to the street, looking out at the passersby while sipping a sparkling water. When she noticed me, she smiled in expectation.

"Hi," I said, taking the chair opposite her. I handed over the plastic bag filled with her neatly folded suit. I took her small designer handbag out of my big blue bag and gave her a pout. "I hate having to give this back."

Her smile took on an edge of seriousness. "You can use it for a while longer. I don't need it right now."

"No, here." I shook the bag. "Take it. It's too small

to fit all my stuff, anyway. It's just the idea of the thing."

She laughed and took it, stowing it carefully before leaning on the table and looking at me. "So…?"

The waiter bustled up, stopping any words from leaving my mouth. He delivered two menus and asked if I wanted a water or drink to start.

"Just a water is fine, thanks," I said.

He gave me a nod and bustled away.

"You turned down Mr. Carlisle." Kimberly gave me a poignant gaze.

"It's for the best. I'm not the type of girl he's looking for."

"And what about the job with Daddy? Did you call?"

"I got home after five on Friday. I'll call first thing tomorrow morning."

She nodded as she sipped her water and opened her menu. "At least you have a job to go to. That's the main thing."

I opened my own menu, looking at the appetizers.

In a nonchalant voice, Kimberly asked, "Did you…?"

"No!" The word was trapped in a hasty release of breath. Heat warmed my cheeks and my body started to tingle, as it always did whenever I thought of his firm and delicious touch.

I wiped my forehead, noticing a sly grin as Kimberly stared at me. I brought my menu up to cover my face. "Somehow, I didn't, no."

I barely saw the top of her red hair shaking slowly. "*How* you said no is beyond me, Olivia Jonston. You are probably the only one. Ever."

I laid the menu down as the waiter came over. Realizing I hadn't actually read the thing, I snatched it back up.

"We need another minute," Kimberly said to the man. Her scrutiny came back to me. "So what happened, exactly. Because no way was I saying no when he tried me out."

"How did he…initiate with you?" I asked in a low voice, rubbing my nose with my finger and half covering my face with my hand at the same time.

Kimberly glanced around, and then lowered her voice. "We went through the interview questions, he brought up some personal items in my life that would fit, and some that might hinder us, and then told me he needed to see if we were physically compatible."

I waited for more.

Kimberly stared for a moment before her brow crumpled. "Isn't that what he said to you? I heard that's his usual way of going about things."

Confused, I sat back. "That's all he said? Because he was pretty…potty-mouthed with me."

An evil glint came to her eyes. "What did he say?"

"I can't believe I am talking about this. Or that I actually—Oh heavens, this is so not my usual…"

"Spill, Olivia! I've always heard he initiates with what he said to me. I'm curious now."

"How do you know…all this when it's supposed to be secret?" I asked to stall her.

"I was asked to interview, just like you. Friends talk…"

I looked at the sky. With a loud exhale to show her I was put out, I gave in. Leaning forward, so *no one* would hear, I said, "He said he wanted to…F me." Her eyes widened. I filled her in with a detailed account of what happened, including how he wanted me to give myself to him.

"Wow," Kimberly breathed, fanning herself like she had in the café the other day. "And you said *no?*"

"It was the *mine* comment." I looked at my menu. "It kind of…crossed a line. I just remember fear coming over me. Then I was running."

Kimberly held her cool glass to her face. "This sounds pervy, but wow, Livy. It also sounds hot. I'd throw myself at him."

"I almost did. He had this soft, commanding voice when he was saying it. It turned my bones to liquid. I can't *believe* I am telling you this."

"It helps to talk about it. An acquaintance of mine had actually been his admin; she's always said he was…like…matter-of-fact about everything. He just took what he needed."

I crinkled my nose. "And she didn't feel used?"

"She got money and connections and everything out of it. And anyway"—Kimberly waved her hand, as if the conversation was off track—"it sounds bad, but he's so good that it doesn't seem robotic at all. My friend *definitely* wasn't complaining. She told me she wished he wanted it more often."

I blew out a breath and stared, unfocused, at my menu. "I don't know that I'd be okay with that. I've been dumped and cheated on enough that a guy just using me for sex like that, without feeling, would probably make me feel…bad. Worthless, kinda."

Kimberly made a sound, like *meh*. "It sounds worse than it is. I mean, when you explained the things he said to you, it sounded way different than how it *felt* when he said them, right?"

I thought back to the aching in my body, and the fire consuming me. Heat coursed through my limbs before pooling in my core, as I remembered the desire in his eyes. The passion.

I noticed a knowing expression. Her lips curled up into a grin.

"Fair enough," I conceded.

With a smug smile, she pushed the menu away. "Plus, you're—" Kimberly's eyes widened, looking over my shoulder. Her mouth rounded into an O.

Wondering if I was about to be mowed down by a runaway bus or something, I glanced over my shoulder.

My stomach rolled.

Hunter Carlisle was striding up the street, his broad shoulders swinging with each step. His button-down shirt didn't have a crease on it. It molded perfectly to those shoulders and hugged his well-defined chest. While he was wearing jeans, they weren't worn like mere jeans; they were more stylish, somehow, fitting his contour and showing off powerful legs.

He came to stop right next to us. "Hello, ladies."

His deep baritone gave me a delicious shiver.

"Hi…" I said. It sounded more like a balloon deflating than a greeting.

His gaze swung to Kimberly. He extended an arm. The leather binder I'd borrowed reached toward her. "I believe this is yours."

"Oh…yes." Kimberly's face was a deep crimson. She gave him a beautiful smile.

Without pausing to gawk at her beauty, like I was doing, he looked back at me. "I wondered if I might have a word?"

My attention was caught in those burning, deep brown eyes, hinting at tousled hair and sex-slicked bodies. It was a very bad idea to be alone with this man. "I was just about to have lunch with Kimberly…"

"Oh, I don't mind. Seriously. At all." Kimberly stood in a rush. Her wood chair squealed behind her as the legs scraped against the ground. "I have somewhere to be, anyway. Livy, honey, call me, okay?" She gave me a poignant look before turning to Hunter, standing much too close for a woman with a boyfriend. She held out her hand and slowed her movements, smiling up at him. "It was a pleasure seeing you again."

I would have to talk to Kimberly about her stance on leaving fallen soldiers behind. She'd abandoned me here with a colossal melter of panties.

I made my way out of the table area and to the sidewalk next to the café.

"Olivia, I would like to have a word with you." I felt Hunter's large, warm hand on my shoulder.

Everything in me *sighed*. My desire to run away like a zombie was chasing me turned into letting him direct me wherever he wanted. My resolve derailed, just like that. How annoying.

We stopped in an alcove beside the restaurant. His intense gaze bored down into me, making it hard to breathe. "Would you have lunch with me?"

I should say no. I really should. I tended to do embarrassing things in his presence, not to mention I completely let down my guard and allowed myself to act in ways I wouldn't normally. But it was Hunter Carlisle. The hottest man alive. Saying no to more time with him seemed ludicrous.

My indecision must've shown on my face, because he said, "I'm not working right now and we'll be in public. You'll be perfectly safe."

Yeah, right. There were many kinds of danger…

"Come with me," he said smoothly. Before I could protest, he led me out of the alcove and to a black luxury car waiting, illegally, by the curb. A large man, who could've played for the NFL based on sheer size alone, got out of the driver's seat and opened the rear door. Hunter handed me into the car. The door closed with the soft *plunk* of luxury.

And just like that, I'd allowed myself to be kidnapped. *Good work resisting…*

I pulled the seatbelt around me as the other rear door opened, admitting Hunter. Only after the car pulled away from the curb did he say, "I wanted to discuss your reservations about working for me."

"How did you find me?"

He stared for a moment, a small crease forming between his eyebrows. He probably realized I was trying to derail that conversation. "I have ways of staying informed."

His tone was serious and self-important, as though he had gone to some extreme measure to track me down. All he'd had to do was check my Facebook page. I'd checked in with Kimberly.

"Okay, then, how did you know that binder was Kimberly's?" I asked.

"You appeared for the second interview dressed like someone with a higher income. While those clothes were pristine, they weren't new. Same with that folder. You have one friend with money, that I've previously met, and were wearing her style. That was purely logic."

A laugh escaped me. "Pure logic, huh? Mr. Private Eye."

The crease in his brow grew larger.

I couldn't help it—I had to poke a little fun. "So your elusive ways to stay informed include social media and label spotting, hmm? I hardly think that makes you a candidate for *Mission: Impossible*. The best you can hope for is *Pink Panther* with this level of intel." I winked.

Fire glimmered in his eyes. "You're challenging me."

He leaned toward me, reducing the space between our bodies. "You have no STDs, which was a chief concern of mine initially, are in excellent health, are using birth control, and run often. Your diet could be better, however."

The smile drained from my face.

"Information—*all* information—is for sale, Olivia. I deal in information as much as I make deals. A sharpshooter has a gun, an arsonist has fire, and I have information. As I said, I research all my second-level applicants. I need to know if there is anything that could damage me in any way. I am a private person, and my admin has the most access. I have to be careful."

I blinked at him, stunned mute.

"You are also nurturing, kind, and levelheaded. Kimberly has the utmost respect for you."

"She talked to you about me?" I blurted. She hadn't said a word about it.

"She had to get permission to recommend you. I admit, I nearly refused, hearing she told you about the position without speaking to my secretary first. But her description intrigued me, especially since people who move in her circles don't generally spend time with those below their tax bracket."

"And that's how you knew about my first boyfriend…" I looked out the window as we crossed the Golden Gate Bridge.

I was leaving the city in the backseat of a car with a man who dealt in secrets. Worse, the driver was a giant, and fighting for my life would be futile. Normally, this would strike me as an appallingly bad idea. In my present state of shock, however, reeling over the extreme breach in privacy, I figured I'd just go with it. If he was ferrying me away to kill me, I'd give him a thumbs-up for preparedness. It would be easier in the long run.

"This comes as a shock to you," he said softly.

I snorted at the gross understatement.

"I forget you aren't accustomed to how I do business. All of the other interviewees keep tabs on me. They expect me to check up on them, and attempt to hide bits of information they'd rather me not discover. I've gotten very good at sussing out the problem areas. With you, however…" He paused for a moment as we turned off the freeway. "Everything was completely in the open. It was refreshing. So honest."

"Well, not exactly out in the *open*, since I assumed the law prevents medical records from wandering out of doctors' offices…"

We turned onto a two-lane road. Trees loomed to either side, the car nearing the national state park. We slowed to a crawl as we turned into a mostly empty parking lot. The driver slid the gear to park and hefted himself from the vehicle. My door opened a moment later.

After we exited the car, Hunter glanced at the bag draped over my shoulder. "You can leave your bag—you won't need it."

I clutched my bag for a moment, deciding. He just

wanted to talk, sure, but the last time we'd met, he'd just wanted to interview me. It ended with his hands in a place they didn't belong, and then me sprinting from the room.

I didn't have high hopes this meeting would go any better.

"I'm fine." I hitched the strap a bit higher on my shoulder.

Hunter's gaze intensified, burning into me. Power emanated from him, the command in his bearing pressuring me. My bones vibrated, wanting to comply. But I knew, without knowing how, that all it would take would be that one yes. Just the one, however trivial, would crush any future resistance. I had to hold out until we finished this meeting and I could get on my way.

My grip tightened and my chin rose. My voice trembled as I repeated, "I'm fine."

Chapter 5

HUNTER GLANCED AT the large man who was standing by my door. Without a word, the man shut the door and moved to the trunk. He removed a large, wheeled suitcase with pockets on the side and front. An extendable handle pulled up from the back. Another piece of luggage came out, this one smaller and with a strap. The man looped it over his shoulder before shutting the trunk.

"We'll be there momentarily," Hunter told his employee.

"Yes, sir, Mr. Carlisle." The man started forward.

"You had questions." Hunter motioned for me to walk, striking up a casual pace in the direction his man had trudged.

"Look, Mr. Carlisle—"

"Hunter, please, when I'm off work."

Was this man ever off work?

"Fine. Hunter. I really appreciate the offer, and I realize it's a highly coveted position, but I think you're wasting your time with me."

"I know exactly what I am doing with you, Olivia."

It felt like champagne bubbled up my insides. My knuckles were white where they gripped my bag. I didn't dare respond—not after the fiasco from the car ride here. I didn't want to know what else he knew.

A few quiet minutes later, we happened upon Hunter's meaty helper placing the last of the food items in an elaborate picnic setup. A white cloth draped across the table. An array of cold cuts spread across what looked like a silver tray. Real silver, too—the kind that needed polishing. And in this case, often got it. Various types of breads adorned another silver tray. A porcelain bowl held a fruit salad, another had potato salad, and a last tray beckoned me closer with chocolate items. A bottle of white wine chilled in a silver canister, and two places were set with finery that might appear on a fancy dinner table.

"How did you fit all this in the suitcase?" I asked in wonder.

"The suitcase looks smaller when Mr. Ramous carries it." His eyes sparkled, but the smile didn't reach his lips.

"I'd wager someone is an excellent packer, too. You're obviously a pro. Do you use this setup to snag love interests, or something?" I belatedly realized how that sounded. "Not that I'm...you know. I didn't mean—"

Hunter's firm touch found the small of my back, directing me forward. "I don't have love interests, Olivia."

He deposited me in front of one of the place settings as the large man, Mr. Ramous, poured me a glass of wine. The liquid glittered in the afternoon sun.

Hunter sat opposite me, focused and intent. "I'd like to hear your questions."

"I don't know that it really matters at this point…"

He continued to stare, waiting.

I sighed in resignation. "Okay, well, Kimberly hadn't mentioned a starting salary. I realize that isn't something an applicant usually asks in an interview, but this isn't a traditional position, so…"

Without balking at the sometimes touchy subject, he answered, "Starting salary is a hundred and thirty thousand a year. You'd start fully vested, which means you have some stock options and the possibility of a bonus at the end of the year."

My heart clattered against my ribcage. Oh what I could do with that much money, living as frugally as I lived. A lot, that was what I could do. I could do an awful lot.

"Benefits would be one of your questions, I am assuming?" Hunter asked. Humor lightened his tone. My glee at that much money probably showed on my face.

"Miss Jonston," Mr. Ramous cut in politely. He stood beside me. "Would you like me to make you a sandwich?"

I blinked at the large man. My mind was still whirling on figures, and new handbags, and a new wardrobe. Oh, and paying school loans—I shouldn't forget that…

"Yes, go ahead, Mr. Ramous," Hunter answered. "Best stick with turkey."

"Yes, sir."

"Benefits, yes," I said in a dream as I imagined telling Jane I was moving to a nicer place. That'd shock her. She thought I was a few weeks away from living on the streets.

Maybe even a designer handbag just so I can fit in with Kimberly's friends once in a while. Those things can't be too expensive, can they? If I just bought one, it wouldn't be terrible…

"We have excellent benefits with very little copay," Hunter said. "Lunch is catered every Friday for office associates, and breakfast every Wednesday. We were voted number three for Best Places to Work in the Bay Area this year, and number five last year. Positions within my company are highly sought after, and our turnover rate is low."

He didn't have to manipulate me; he was showering me in perks and greenbacks. The other job didn't come close to *any* of this. I'd hardly be able to live on its salary, the benefits weren't super, and the lunchroom was barely stocked with coffee…

Mr. Ramous put a sandwich on my plate. Without asking, he spooned a heap of potato salad next to it. I let him, desperately trying to remember those hard-hitting questions I'd prepared for the interview.

"Work hours?" I asked hesitantly.

"I work long hours, as you probably know. I require

my admin to start at nine, sharp. Sometimes she's able to leave at six, and often she can leave for a lunch break. It's more usual, however, that she leave closer to eight. She might work one of the weekend days, but get at least one day off unless in dire circumstances." Hunter stopped talking and glanced at Mr. Ramous. "That'll be all, Mr. Ramous. I'll text you when we're through."

"Yes, sir."

Mr. Ramous started walking toward the car. When he was out of sight, Hunter's deep brown eyes came back to me. "In a usual situation, I would generally require one day a week, approximately a half-hour to one hour, for sexual activity. I rarely demand more, and I ensure pleasure is both given and received. I don't respond to sexual advances from my admins, and would consider it a breach of contract if she continued to give them after a light warning. If I don't satisfy her sex drive, I ask that she fulfill it elsewhere. When I cannot deny my own urges, I seek her out."

The buzz of a bee floated by. Leaves rattled, disturbed by the light breeze.

The man had given me a staring problem.

"But your fiancé…" I said, trying to ignore the heat in my body.

"Has also signed a contract. Our situation is a truce with my father and an alliance with her family. We lead entirely separate lives."

I shook myself out of my stupor before leaning back. This was all just nuts. He was doing a great job of selling his proposed situation like it was completely normal—like everyone had contracts allowing their boss to get grabby—but I wasn't buying it. He was bat-shit crazy. No two ways about it.

I glanced away to the side, pulling my attention away from him. It was time for the eject button. "While the money does sound great, and I wouldn't care about the hours, I do care about other things. I'll be taking another job, but thank you for going through all the trouble to answer my questions."

"If you're talking about the IT position in McCannon Industries, that position has been put on hold for the foreseeable future. There is no other job, Olivia. I'm what you've got."

My world bled of color for a moment as what he said sank in. "What do you mean, it's *on hold*?"

He took a sip of his wine before answering. "We both know that that position would neither challenge you, nor pay you fairly. It's a waste of your talent. Please listen to my offer. If you then decide it isn't for you, I can place you in a position elsewhere in my company. There's no reason to waste your time with companies like McCannon."

I pushed my plate away, bracing my hands against the table. "First of all, that's none of your business. You don't get to decide how I spend my time. And second, I've heard your offer, Hunter. I heard it, I felt it, and I rejected it."

Those smoldering eyes hardened. "That was a standard offer. I'm prepared to offer you a trial period. One month, Olivia. One month with no personal contract whatsoever, except for the secrecy clause. I will ask the usual hours, but I will not touch you. This will be purely professional, like my relationship with Brenda. At the end of that month, you can decide if the benefits will be worth that personal contract. If not, then we'll discuss where else in the company you'd rather be placed. You'll receive pay as though my admin for that month, but if you choose to go elsewhere, we can talk about pay scales and benefits at that time for the various positions that interest you.

"I consider this an extremely generous offer, one that I've never made to anyone else. I want you, Olivia. And yes, part of me wants to touch you. I want to hear you whisper my name when you give in to your desires. But I can ignore that if it means you'll give this job a try. Just a try. It isn't so much to ask."

He paused, heat and determination in his eyes. He leaned toward me possessively. "Will you work for me?"

My heart thumped, begging me to give in. Desire warred with logic. Lust overshadowed coherent thought.

The tug of his charisma couldn't be ignored. It sucked me in. I was lost.

"Yes," I heard myself whisper.

Chapter 6

On Monday I walked into that large, stately high rise for the third time. This time when I checked in, it was as an employee. Hunter Carlisle's employee.

I didn't know if this was a good idea, but it was done now. I didn't have any other options—he'd made sure of that. And while in personal life, I might've been angry, in business, I wasn't surprised. He'd outmaneuvered me, plain and simple. He probably did it all the time in his profession, and if I ever wanted to climb the ladder, or get back at him, I'd have to start paying attention.

I approached Brenda with a hesitant step and a tight hold on my trusty blue bag. She glanced up when I got close, looked back at her computer, clicked the mouse a few times, then stood. "Welcome, Miss Jonston—may I call you Olivia?"

"Yes, of course. Or Livy."

She nodded and swung her hand toward the desk next to hers. "Have a seat. And congratulations. You've landed a highly sought after position. I expect great things from you." She stepped around her desk and shooed me into mine.

I put my bag down as I sat into my new seat. Waiting until I was comfortable, she continued, "Mr. Carlisle mentioned you'd probably want two monitors?"

"Oh." I looked at the moderate-sized screen in front of me. I'd never had a real job before, so in truth, I had no idea what I needed.

Brenda must've noticed my blank look, because her lips pursed. "We'll get you two." She pointed at the sleek, brand-new laptop sitting in the middle of the desk. "That is set up with your user ID and password. The computer bag is behind you—Mr. Carlisle said you might like to work remotely on occasion, or take your work home. I'd have to advise you to be careful with that. He's demanding, and he'll ask for everything you have. If you don't learn the word 'no,' he'll work you into the ground."

She was a little too late with that advice. "Got it." I gave her a thumbs-up.

She returned the sentiment with a tight smile. Possibly the thumbs-up was a little weird. "Get yourself settled, and then report to Mr. Carlisle."

I wished, just once, the butterflies, tingles, or shivers wouldn't overrun me when I heard Hunter's name. Just one time.

I busied myself setting up my computer. That done, I checked over the pens, which I hoped I wouldn't have to use very often, and took a quick glance at the company intranet. Hunter's flawless face popped up immediately with the title "A Note from the CEO." Unlike most CEO portraits, he wasn't smiling. He didn't need to. It seemed like he was staring out of the picture, directly at me. He was as photogenic as he was charismatic. I couldn't tear my eyes away.

Some things just weren't fair.

I was just about to lock my screen and search for a notepad when an instant message popped up.

Hunter Carlisle: *Good morning.*

"Good God!" I yanked my hands away from the keyboard as though his head had popped out of the screen like a poltergeist.

"You okay?" Brenda asked, walking toward my desk with two coffee mugs. I hadn't even noticed that she'd left.

"Oh yeah. Sure. Ha." I leaned toward the computer. Hopefully she'd lose interest in my ridiculousness if she thought I was working. Regardless that I had nothing to work on.

Olivia Jonston: *Hi.*

Olivia Jonston: *Good morning.*

Hunter Carlisle: *When you have a chance, come in here.*

Olivia Jonston: *Yes, sir.*

"Here you go." Brenda set a full cup of coffee down in front of me.

"Oh. Thanks."

She gave me another tight smile. "That's for Mr. Carlisle. One of your duties is to take him coffee. I get him a cup when I refill mine, and his assistant takes it in."

"Oh." I wanted to ask why we needed an assembly line for a cup of coffee, but thought better of it. I didn't need to get fired on my first day.

I grabbed a notepad and pen, and then the cup. "Great."

Walking into his office, nervousness ate away my insides. My new boss sat behind his desk, broad and handsome. His face was set in a stern mask as he typed, completely focused on his task.

I stopped at the edge of his desk and held out his coffee. "Brenda wanted me to give you this…"

He glanced up. Those sexy eyes took me in for a brief moment before noticing the mug. "Just put it down and have a seat."

His desk had three neat piles of paper, a few items that I'd previously knocked to the ground, and his computer stuff.

I eyed the legs of the visitor chairs. Knowing me, I'd be distracted by something, trip on one of those chair legs, and dowse his desk with coffee. Bad idea. Taking the safe way out, I put his mug on the corner where it was likely to do the least amount of damage. Then I sat down.

"I wanted to explain the loose structure of this office," he started, clicking his mouse before turning to me. "You, as the administrative assistant, report to me. I will give you instruction directly, or I will pass you off to Brenda, who is my executive assistant, for instruction. At the moment, you two are not equal. She has years of experience working with me, and knows her job inside and out. In the future, if you get to grips with your job, and take on more, I'm sure you two will level out. That's my hope, anyway. Regardless, you're both integral to this operation, and you are both—or will be—on an equal footing as far as I am concerned. Is that clear?"

I tapped my notebook with the tip of my pen and frowned. "Yes." Seemed pretty logical so far.

"What's the problem?"

My brows shot up and my eyes widened. I stammered, "N-nothing."

"Did your frown mean you have a problem with answering to Brenda?"

I felt like I'd been caught stealing. "Not at all, no! The delivery was just so heavy-handed. She has a higher title, so the fact that we'd eventually be equal was unexpected."

His shoulders relaxed just a little. "I've had problems with admins treating Brenda as a subservient member of my staff. I don't want that to happen with you."

I bobbed my head in understanding.

"Today you'll be doing menial tasks—copying, filing, getting coffee."

"Great." I quietly tapped my pen. I was getting a

huge paycheck—I'd shine Brenda's boots if he wanted me to.

"Brenda has a list for you to do, and you can address any questions to her. When you're finished, check in here again. I'll have something for you."

"Okey-dokey."

"Questions?"

"Nope. I think I got it."

He looked at me silently. I felt the heat rush to my face before spreading through my body, basking in that sexy look of hooded, smoldering eyes. If I'd signed that contract, he could ask me to stand right now, lean over the desk, and—

"Are you okay?"

"What?" I stood in a rush, clutching the notepad to my chest. "Sorry. Is that all?"

He continued to stare. Apparently his "you're excused" was a silent one.

"So...no, then." I paused in a half-turn to indicate I was leaving, just to be sure. His face didn't so much as twitch.

"Right," I mumbled as I finished the turn with a hot face. A "goodbye," or even "get out," wouldn't go amiss. It would cut down on the time I spent remembering his hard body pressed against mine. Or my crazy yet insistent desire to have him take me right there.

What have I done taking this job?

IT TURNED OUT Brenda's "list" was three sheets of paper

filled with menial tasks. She showed me where the copy machine was, pointed out the conference room, and then gave me a quick tour of the kitchen. Being at the top of the building, the floor was more a suite than anything, and we were the only people in it. It made things a lot quieter than I expected.

After I finished the first task of making copies, I carried the stack of desecrated trees to Brenda. I couldn't help an offhanded comment about digital files. It would save so much time.

I could tell her first impulse was to ignore me. I wouldn't have minded—my mother had made an art out of ignoring me, so I was used to it. As she took the gigantic stack, though, she slowed. Thoughtfully, she looked at me over her glasses. "Digital files, huh? What would be involved in that?"

My confusion was probably written all over my face. "You mean… Like… Sorry, what do you mean? Like how do you do it?"

Brenda dropped the stack next to the file cabinets and straightened up, surveying me. "You said it would save time…?"

"Well…yeah." I cocked a hip. I felt like we were speaking a different language. My education had led me to believe this was common knowledge. "I mean, you have to scan it if it isn't already a digital file, which is largely the same as copying it, but you can do that right to the file, right? And then, after that, you just…have it in a file."

"But we'd both need access…" She let her words linger.

"So, yeah, you just label it, put it in a file we both have access to on the public drive so the company has a backup, and Bob's your uncle. No more filing by hand."

"Hmm." Brenda wrote something down on a Post-it. "You just gave yourself something to do."

I nearly sighed. I should've expected that. Talk about menial, mind-numbing tasks…

AT FIVE O'CLOCK, after I'd crossed off the last of Brenda's wish list, I dragged myself into Hunter's office. My mind was numb, it felt like drool coated the side of my face, and my eyes were sandy with fatigue. As I approached Hunter's desk, I noticed the last cup of coffee I had brought him sat untouched at the corner of his desk.

A slight frown creased Hunter's features as he absently chewed on the end of a pen. My gaze dipped to those lush lips, parted slightly to allow in the black plastic.

"Sir," I said softly, my gaze moving to the light stubble on his chin.

His face shifted, drawing my stare to his eyes. His frown cleared and fatigue took its place. "Yes. Olivia."

I continued to stare, hypnotized by those entrancing, smoldering eyes. They looked like he'd just walked out of a bedroom where a satisfied woman lay dozing.

"Olivia?"

"Oh." I shook myself out of my stupor. "Sorry. I haven't used my brain much today. It hasn't come back online yet."

He fell back into his seat. The dwindling light glowed through the windows behind him. He glanced at his computer. Light surprise lit up his features. "It's late—you took much longer than I expected to get through Brenda's list…"

I scoffed. "I added work without meaning to."

His brows climbed in a question. I elaborated: "I recommended a couple things that would save time in the long run. Unfortunately, it also wasted—um, took my time today to set up."

"Such as?"

"Electronic filing, rearranging some spreadsheets, a more effective mailing list—rudimentary things like that."

"Did you eat lunch?"

"Huh?" I couldn't keep up with the quick change in topic.

"Did you eat lunch?" he asked again, rising.

"No?"

"You're not sure?" There was a smile in his voice as he shrugged into his jacket.

I watched the play of muscle across his shoulders. If I signed that contract I'd be able to see those without his shirt, I'd bet…

"C'mon. I'll buy you dinner," he said, hopefully not noticing the hunger in my eyes. His hand found the small of my back as he guided me out of the office.

Without thinking, I leaned into the touch. Into his

heat. His delicious smell, of expensive cologne mixed with masculinity, wound around my senses. His muscle moved against my side, so hard.

My body lit up. My core pooled fire. I wanted to stop and turn to him. To run my hands up his chest before stripping away his shirt.

Get a grip!

In desperation, I peeled myself from his side. "Excuse me," I said in a breathy voice. "My brain is on hiatus."

"It's no problem." His voice sounded husky. Deeper. I took his hand away.

I wiped my forehead as we entered the elevator, willing my soggy brain to get in gear and stop letting my libido have control. At this rate, I'd commit a cardinal sin by the end of the week!

When we emerged into the encroaching night outside the building, his hand found the small of my back again. Strangely, his firm touch felt comfortable. Safe and reassuring. It felt the exact opposite of what he really was. I couldn't move away.

He steered me across the street and down the block to a busy Italian eatery. We stopped in front of the opened door. A small crowd of people waited just inside at the hostess desk. A couple of groups lined the front of the building, no doubt waiting for their table.

"Looks packed," I said.

Hunter didn't acknowledge my words. Instead, he steered me through the door and stepped around the small hostess podium into the space of the young woman. Her eyes flashed and a smile curled her lips when she saw him. After saying a few words, which were lost to the buzz of the restaurant, he stepped back.

"Five minutes," he said when he rejoined me. The hostess' gaze had followed him, the smile being replaced with a scowl as his hand resumed its position on my back. "Would you like to wait outside?"

"But what about everyone else?" I asked quietly.

He barely glanced around as he steered me outside. He loosened his tie, not hiding a tired sigh.

"Long day?" I asked, once again standing too close. I couldn't help it.

"We have a possible merger on the table. There are a lot of moving parts and long-term effects."

"Not buying a company, but a merger?" I crossed my arms, aware that a group of three women were sending us furtive glances. My faded black skirt and out-of-style blouse didn't fit with this upscale crowd.

"Yes, exactly. I have an eye on a buyout that would negate the merger, and be better for the company long-term, but my competition is…steep. The board is less than thrilled."

"Oh. Mhm." I didn't have the brainpower for business-speak. I needed a sandwich.

"Mr. Carlisle?" The hostess stepped out of the restaurant and flashed Hunter a stunning smile. "We're ready for you."

The hostess gave us menus as we sat down, flashed another winning smile that Hunter ignored, and moved away.

Hunter pushed his menu to the side. "How was your first day?"

"Good. Okay." I glanced down at the menu and tried not to show my shock that a ravioli dish went for thirty-five dollars. No way was it worth that much.

I pushed the menu to the side, only then noticing Hunter staring at me. "A little boring," I finally admitted.

"Tomorrow we'll get you started on some other things," he said in an easy tone.

The waiter showed up to take our orders. When he was gone, Hunter's fixed look traveled over my face. Uneasiness crossed his visage before he looked away to the side, seemingly at the window across the restaurant.

Not wanting to sit in silence, I reached for small talk. "How long have you been CEO?"

"Two years."

"And before that?"

"I graduated at twenty and was placed in a junior vice president position by my father." His tone grew hard. He looked away to the distant window again. "In my situation, you would've rejected his handout, I'm sure, but I knew he was the fastest way to the top. From there, I leveraged various achievements and positions until I fought for the job I have. They worried about placing someone so young—for good reason, of course. And my decisions, which are generally thought extremely progressive, are constantly questioned."

"You graduated college early."

Hunter's head snapped back as his look colored with confusion and humor both. He gave a light snort as the waiter delivered two glasses of wine. I had no idea what was funny. "Yes. I was homeschooled through high school and entered college a couple years early."

"Wow. Smart." I bobbed my head. "If my mom had turned up a week ago offering me a job or money, I would've had my hand out so fast it'd fly off my wrist."

I took a sip of my wine. "Oh, that's good." I swirled the liquid in my glass as he tasted his. I searched my brain for something to talk about. I knew absolutely nothing about this guy. I didn't even know where to start. "So, how about those Niners, huh? New stadium. You been?"

His lips tweaked upward. "I have, yes, but they are on a losing streak."

"Oh." I took another sip of my wine, unperturbed. "That's a waste of a new stadium, then."

"So it would seem."

I mimicked a stuffy English accent. "Yes, yes. Quite." I did a little facial gymnastics for no real reason other than he wouldn't stop staring. It seemed no one had informed him how rude that was. "You a big sports buff?"

"Not really. I catch the important games, but don't have a vested interest in who wins."

"Business related, huh? Have to schmooze with the execs?"

"Yes, exactly."

I nodded, glancing around. "You come here often?"

Before he could answer, the food showed up, carried by a bustling waiter.

"Oh. That was fast," I mumbled, leaning back so my plate could be placed in front of me.

"This establishment is known for their speedy turnaround time. With a mostly business clientele, they need to keep things moving."

I sampled my ravioli, and then moaned as the interesting and distinct flavors rolled around in my mouth. I ate another, sitting back in my chair and savoring the delicious dish. I'd been as good as dieting for the last four months, eating cheap and light, trying to save money. This was a treat I didn't want to ruin with social etiquette.

Only after I was halfway through did I come out of my food fog.

"Wow." I landed a direct stare at Hunter. He had been watching me with that crease between his eyebrows. It seemed my level of crazy didn't turn up in his background checks. "This is something special."

"Yes." A smile threatened his shapely lips. He looked down at his dish. "They are consistently above par."

"You can say that again." I watched him cut a piece of steak. "Bite?"

His fork paused next to his mouth.

I continued to stare expectantly.

"Of my…" His hand jerked and the cutest expression came over his face. He looked like a young boy who'd been bedazzled by a strange neighborhood girl—off-kilter and a little terrified.

The bite on the end of his fork hovered for a moment before drifting across the table. His eyes were sparkling and the edge of his lips quirked, threatening a smile. Apparently not many people forced him to share.

I reached for the fork, but he pulled back a little, clearly staking his claim on the utensil. He probably thought I would refuse to give it back until I'd eaten all his dinner. He was probably right.

I leaned forward with my mouth open, letting him deposit the morsel on my tongue. The sauce flirted with my taste buds immediately, and then exploded in my mouth as I chewed the stake.

"Ooo mmm guud," I said with a mouthful. I rolled my eyes and leaned back, chewing with delight. After I swallowed, I smiled at him. "So good."

He dropped his hand to the table. "Do you want another?"

I gave him a sheepish smile. "No, I have mine. Want a bite?"

His immediate reaction was to shake his head, but he hadn't looked away. That indicated curiosity. Cue food pushing.

I speared a ravioli and shoved it through the air. "Try it. Seriously. You won't regret it."

He glanced around the restaurant before looking back at me. His brows settled low over his eyes. He didn't lean forward.

"Have you had this dish before?" I asked, pushing the fork forward just a bit farther.

His look intensified, uncomfortable and wary at the same time. I almost relented, but something made me keep my hand out. Made me keep pushing. He always seemed so controlled. So boxed in. I wanted him to be unsettled like he always made me, and I knew I could because I wasn't under his control like all the other admins. I was the wild card.

"C'mon, live a little." I wiggled my fork.

Without breaking eye contact, he leaned forward and closed his mouth over the bite. His lips slid along the fork slowly, drawing my eyes. My mind started buzzing as I homed in on the little bit of orange at the corner of his mouth. Everything in my person wanted to lick it off before fastening my lips to his in a needy taste.

One of my shoulders ticked upward. I had no idea why, other than my body was uncomfortably tight. I felt another hot flash coming on.

"So anyway, uh...how many days do you work?" I asked. I needed to change the subject. To dislodge his intent, focused stare.

"Seven."

"Yikes. No breaks, huh? All work and no play makes Jack a very dull boy." I speared another piece of ravioli.

"Sometimes that's best. Being dull." Finally his gaze dipped, leaving me.

I sucked in a deep breath. I kind of wanted to comment, or ask why he needed to work so much, but I no longer wanted to try and get to know him. The man was gorgeous, and he had a hold on me. I didn't want to learn he was also interesting. That way led to signing a contract, or worse, losing my heart. The last person on earth I should lose my heart to was this man. I didn't need his warning to know that, either. I just needed to watch the female eyes in the room. They always found him.

Yes, Hunter Carlisle was very dangerous. Best to steer clear.

We finished our meal fairly quickly. Afterward, Hunter walked me to the corner and stopped. He faced me. "How will you get home?"

"Bus." I glanced down the street. "They come pretty regularly."

"I'll have my driver take you."

"No, I'm okay." I waved away the offer and stepped in the direction of the bus stop. "I've been living in the city for four months—I'm well familiar with the bus system."

His tone deepened. "It's late and the streets are dangerous." He stepped closer, his body looming over me, his physical presence dominating my space. I felt the electric buzz of his proximity. "I'll have you taken home."

I stared up into those deep brown eyes and felt my resolve weaken. His arm came around me, possessive and commanding. His hand settled on the familiar place on my back. Not able to help myself, I leaned into him, my hand bracing on his hard chest.

"Yes, okay," I said quietly. He'd won another battle. If I didn't stop saying yes, he'd win the war and make me his. I couldn't let that happen.

Chapter 7

BRENDA WAS READY for me with another piece of paper when I arrived at work the next day. I had barely settled into my chair before she was laying it on my desk along with the cup of coffee for Hunter.

"You can't possibly have more filing," I pleaded, picking up the paper.

She snorted as she moved back to her seat. "No, no more filing. I let Mr. Carlisle know that you didn't complain once yesterday—I think that's a record."

I glanced over the lengthy list. It seemed mostly composed of various articles of clothing.

"I think you gave me the wrong thing," I said, glancing at my email as soon as my computer booted up. I had one item of company propaganda and a lot of blank space.

My instant messenger pinged.

Hunter Carlisle: *Good morning. Come to my office.*

"Please," I muttered under my breath to finish his

sentence for him. The man could do with some lessons on etiquette.

"That's the right one," Brenda said, settling into her chair. "You'll see."

Frowning at her, because I didn't like that last comment, I dropped the paper, picked up the coffee and a notepad, and made my way into Hunter's office. When I got about halfway, he glanced up from his desk, clean-shaven and bright eyed. He held up something as I neared.

"What's that?" I asked, placing his coffee at the corner of his desk before bending forward to take the piece of plastic I recognized as a credit card.

"My company card. When you sign on—"

"If," I interrupted absently.

His eyes turned sharp. "*When* you sign on, you'll get a permanent one."

My mouth turned into a duckbill as I held the card, thinking of what he'd need that I'd have to run out for. He continued, "You are to take the day to find suitable attire for someone working in my office."

Insecurity created a tightness in my chest. I glanced down at my unflattering pink blouse and gray skirt.

Hunter must've seen my reaction, because he said, "This is a perk of the job. This is not specific to you, though I'm sure you'll appreciate it the most. Brenda will give you a list of items I usually ask that my admins wear. Some of those items…will not be necessary with our current arrangement. However, if you want to update your lingerie, you may take advantage of it."

I flushed, but remained silent.

"There is a list of retailers I prefer you use. If you choose to shop outside of those retailers, please make sure the quality is comparable. After today, any time you feel you need work clothes, feel free to use that card. Likewise, any time you need transportation, which does not include the bus, use that card. Save your receipts and turn them into Brenda. She will not review your purchases unless she thinks you're abusing the privilege, so don't feel embarrassed about whatever items of clothing you might need. Questions?"

I shook my head dumbly, half excited to go on a shopping spree, and half self-conscious of my current wardrobe.

"And buy yourself a new handbag—I can't bear to look at that blue monstrosity." He glanced away toward his computer, but before I lost sight of his face, I saw the small smile curving his lips.

"It's a very handy bag," I said with faux disdain as I turned for the door.

"And Olivia…" I looked back. "Go wild. I can afford it."

With my seemingly constant red face, I walked out to my desk and picked up the piece of paper. To Brenda I said, "Do you get to buy clothes on the company dime?"

"On Mr. Carlisle's dime, yes. He's picky. Works for me. I'll take free clothes any day."

"He said company card," I muttered as I noticed his name across the plastic.

"I'm sure he finds a way to write it off, but that's his personal account. He has others, of course—this is the one he uses for us. Take it, darling. He can afford it."

I shut down my computer and grabbed my blue monstrosity. With a sly grin, I said, "Who am I to argue?"

"Exactly."

"I guess I'll see you tomorrow, then." I gave her a small wave as I walked by her desk.

"Yep. And good work yesterday. You really helped me out. I hate doing that stuff."

Her laughter followed me down the hall toward the elevator. I couldn't help but chuckle along with her.

THE DAY PASSED in a whir of extravagance. The list of retailers was all top of the line and extremely expensive. I would never, and I mean *never*, shop at those places with my own money, even if this was my job forever and I was making a ton of money. Five hundred dollars for a shirt? A thousand for slacks? Outrageous. But Hunter said spend, and Brenda said I had better shut up and just do it, so here I was, charging two grand for the first store alone.

First I bought just the plain essentials—skirts, pants (which was okay, since I hadn't signed that personal contract), and blouses. But as the day wore on, I thought more and more of my appearance and my situation, and the fact that I never really let go. I didn't hide within my clothes, but I didn't flaunt it, either. My body wasn't rock star, but I did have some curve, and I did have some cleavage. With my cheap-food diet these last four months, I was also smaller than I'd been in a few years. Why not let loose a little?

"You know what, do you have anything…a little sexier?" I asked the overanxious saleslady with my customary red face.

She gave me a sly smile. "Absolutely."

After we roamed the store a second time while I blushed so often the red probably looked painted on, I paid the bill and decided to head for home. Only…I didn't really have any good lingerie. Most of my panties were cotton and boring. My bras supported me fine, but were drab.

I bit my lip and thought about what Hunter had said. I didn't need to buy them for him, but I could still buy them for me. And I needed some new stuff—wearing cute and sexy lingerie every once in a while made a girl feel special. Made her feel as sexy as the black lace hugging her body. I hadn't had that feeling in a very long time.

Why not? He can afford it.

Without another thought, I took off to the final store, intending to buy all the things I'd looked at over the years but backed away from because they were too expensive.

Watch out world, Olivia has someone else's credit

card!

THE NEXT DAY I showed up wearing one of the plainer outfits, a silk blouse in mauve with a pinstriped skirt. I came around my desk as Brenda walked into the area with two cups of coffee.

"Oh, you're here. Great. Here you go." She set the coffee cup on my desk.

I dropped my stuff, including an extremely cute, and seriously expensive, new handbag, and held my breath as I reached for the coffee. As expected, Brenda glanced at my outfit.

"You look nice." She sipped her coffee as she made her way to her chair.

I felt my brow climb toward my hairline as I waited for more. Maybe a comment on the quality. Or the cost.

When she ignored me so she could check her email, I figured that was it. Hopefully, that also meant I was in the clear.

So far, so good.

I turned on my computer and picked up the cup of coffee. I pushed open the door and walked into the room with an even step, trying to act like I dressed in thousands of dollars worth of clothing every day.

Hunter sat at his desk, handsome as ever. He glanced up when I neared, gave me a brief once-over, and said, "How did you get to work today?"

I stuttered in my step with the unexpected question and nearly sloshed the coffee all over his desk. I jerked the cup away from important papers, and then to the side, worried there'd be backsplash and I'd get some on my new clothes. The scorching liquid splashed over the side of the cup and dripped down my hand.

"Ow!" I set the cup on the floor before shaking out my hand.

"Here." Hunter jumped up, ripped off his jacket, and held it out to my hand.

"No!" I screeched, yanking my hand away as the burning subsided into red, inflamed skin. "You probably paid thirty grand for that jacket!"

"It's just money, Olivia," he said, reaching. "Give me your hand."

The deep-toned command dripped down my back pleasantly. I slowed in my movements, allowing him to take my arm. The silk of the inside of his jacket came around my hand and wrist to wipe off the moisture.

I closed my eyes at his touch. Felt his fingers curled around my upper arm and the warmth from his nearness seeping through my blouse and lacy white bra. My nipples constricted as he pulled away his jacket to look at the damage.

A soft tug on my arm had me willingly following him around his desk. He yanked open his top drawer. A couple squares of foil caught the sun.

Condoms.

My sex swelled and my breathing turned heavy. I willed him to grab one of those. I wanted him to bend me over the desk, my flaming skin be damned. But his hand reached over and pulled out a package of wet wipes instead.

Items used for cleanup.

I wanted him to fuck me.

"Oh God," I breathed, squeezing my eyes shut as my fierce desire warred with logic.

Please initiate something, Hunter. I'll say yes right here, consequences be damned.

"This'll make it feel better." His deep tone rumbled through my body. His touch danced across the skin on my arm. The wipe cooled my burning skin.

My sex pounded, craving attention.

"Hunter," I whispered.

His movements slowed. His fingers, checking my wound, stilled.

I looked up and met those deep brown eyes, intent. His gaze roamed my face before resting on my lips. I thought he might bend down and kiss me. Just to see what I tasted like. But his brow furrowed and wariness crossed his features.

He stepped back. "I think you're okay now."

I breathed out as cold washed over me, replacing his warmth. I blinked into his withdrawal, feeling the pain crawl back into my arm. The light from the window made me squint as my brain floated back into control.

"Oy," I said as I took a deep breath. "Okay." Still dazed, I turned to go.

"Olivia?"

"Yeah?"

He flung his jacket across one of the visitor chairs before rolling up his sleeves past his muscular forearms. "I assume you took the bus this morning…"

I blinked, willing my brain to shake off the desire turning my thoughts to molasses. "Yes?"

"I have a car service. Use it or take a cab. There is no need for you to be taking the filthy bus."

"Sure." I didn't bother arguing that cabs were as filthy as any bus. Billionaires didn't really understand the lives of the average city-dweller. "Is that all, sir?"

My hand was starting to throb now that I didn't have the distraction of Hunter beating down on me. It was good. Pain helped the brain focus.

"I like the new look. It suits you."

He didn't bother looking up to deliver the compliment, but it was a compliment all the same. I beamed, thankful I hadn't gotten the wrong thing. "Thank you."

"Bring me another cup of coffee in a few minutes."

My beam turned into a frown. My tone hinted at the expression as I said, "Anything else, sir?"

"No, you can go."

My frown deepened. "A thank you wouldn't kill you," I muttered under my breath as I walked back out to my desk. Once there, I said to Brenda, "Do we have anything for burns? I spilled coffee."

"There's a medicine cabinet in the kitchen. Make some coffee while you're there."

"Does no one know the power of thank you in this place?" I trudged off to the kitchen.

THE NEXT COUPLE of days passed by in a blur. I had my nose in spreadsheets, looking over Hunter's schedules so I knew what was going on, and learning the ropes. I had to learn more about the company, the product, the people who came to see him often—lots of things to get familiar with. Brenda was super helpful and patient, and Hunter ignored me most of the time, just like he did her, so things were starting to be like a normal, highly stressful, but well-paying job. I was actually liking it.

I only had the month, though. Hunter had made that clear. At the end of the month, regardless of if I liked this setup, my time would run out. I'd either need to dive into the naughty pool to keep the job I liked, or step away from the ledge and try to find something else. Only time would tell.

When Saturday rolled around, I was standing in front of my closet biting my lip in indecision. I'd worn three black skirts in a row, with conservative, airy blouses. I'd really love to wear some jeans, and thought really hard about wearing pants, but one was forbidden and the others were also black.

"No more black," I murmured at my closet.

I pushed aside yet another black skirt, wondering if I'd been thinking of death when I was shopping, and walked my fingers over pink fabric. Then white. And finally hovered on red. Easily the shortest skirt, it hugged my butt and thighs just right. I had a tightfitting, cleavage-showing white shirt to go with it. The saleslady had *raved* about how fabulous I looked in the outfit. She was just *gaga* over it.

I glanced at the pink skirt, something a bit longer and not so…red as the other selection. But that brazen fabric kept drawing my eye. And it was Saturday—Brenda wouldn't be there… I could totally get away with something a bit wilder. Plus, since Hunter barely glanced up at me anymore, and I'd probably just be at my desk on the computer the whole day, no one would really see…

With an evil smile, I took the skirt down and then the shirt. I tossed them on my bed and opened my underwear drawer. The black lacy bra and panty set nearly jumped into my hand, since black and red so obviously went together, but I grabbed the white set instead. I was breaking from the norm in dress, so why not in what I would usually put together, too?

Then, because I absolutely couldn't help myself, I pulled out the white garter.

"I cannot believe I am doing this!" It felt like Halloween.

I put the garter on first before realizing I needed the panties. I was definitely a novice at this. The stockings were a pain, especially with my nails, but I got them hooked in and all set. I stepped into the skirt, and finally put on my shirt. After I was set, I stepped in front of the full-length mirror.

My stomach squirmed in unease as I looked over my curves, on display for the world to see. My breasts and hips waved hello. Even my legs drew notice, the gloss of the stockings—or were they nylons?—showing their shape.

I blew out a breath as I turned to survey the back. A black line crawled up the center of each leg until it ducked under my skirt.

Frowning, I ran my finger along it. Sewn into the tights, it was a style that should've probably been worn with another piece of black in the attire. I wore red and white. So…no longer matching.

I thought about the effort to change into another pair of tights. Nope. Not going to happen. Way too much work. I'd just make sure to keep my front to Hunter while speaking, and walk away quickly. Hopefully he wouldn't notice.

I faced front again and smoothed my hands over the skirt.

I felt completely exposed. Completely. *I should take this off and wear the pants…*

I stopped myself from acting. I was doing this. I was going to wear this in public, and then hide in the office before wearing it in public again on the way home. People would look, and I knew that, but I was going to hold my head high, and not be so self-conscious about showing the outline of my body. After all, this was short and tight for me, but girls my age wore things that showed their butt cheeks. I was still in the respectable zone. Mostly.

Sticking to my guns, I grabbed some heels—black, both because they matched that weird seam, and also because that was all I had—and headed to the bathroom. After hair and makeup, I walked out the front door with a light coat, belatedly realizing I was supposed to call that danged car service Brenda kept on at me about. It was too late now, though, and there wasn't a cab in sight.

The bus it was.

I got to the office amid a few stares and only one cat-call. It was actually way less than I anticipated, which meant this outfit was nowhere near the scandal I had expected. The guard barely glanced up as I stalked through, and no one was there to witness me in the elevator.

Anticlimactic.

I booted up my computer at 9:01 a.m. and glanced beside me. Hunter's door was slightly ajar, which meant he was inside. I checked my emails, saw a few from him with tasks for the day, and was about to respond to a question about a spreadsheet when the instant message pinged.

Hunter Carlisle: *Good morning. Bring in coffee.*

The man was busy, sure, but also a touch lazy. It had to be acknowledged.

Olivia Jonston: *Sure thing. Be there in a sec.*

I stared at the screen for a moment. And nope, just as I expected—no thank you.

"Lazy and rude," I muttered, trudging off to the kitchen.

That was another thing I needed to learn—walking properly in a skirt and heels. Trudging was for hoodies and jeans. You didn't trudge through the office in a position of power. You stalked. Or marched. Or…walked. I'd settle for walking, which was not easy to do gracefully in three-inch heels, no matter what the fashion models and Kimberly might ask me to believe.

After I got the coffee and slowed to a trudging sort of lurch so I didn't spill, I set my cup down and went in to deliver his. I put it down in the usual spot before straightening up.

He was staring at me.

Giving him a slight scowl, I waited to hear what the problem was. When nothing came, I raised my brow in expectation. Usually he just came out and told me what he wanted—this silent staring thing wasn't helpful. I would think it was my outfit, or the way I was walking, but his gaze didn't leave my eyes.

Finally, unimpressed he couldn't read my facial sign language, I asked, "What?"

"You have your instructions for today?"

"I saw you emailed, yes."

"And do you have any questions?"

I swiped my hair out of my face, wishing I'd brought a clip. "I haven't reviewed it yet."

"Let me know." He turned back to his computer.

"Yes, sir," I said automatically as I turned. I practiced my walk, confident in his focus on his work and therefore not looking. The heels gave me a lot of hip movement, which was probably fine—my booty wasn't big enough to take out small children as I walked by— but I still walked too much on my toes.

At the door, I snapped as I remembered lunch and turned back around. Hunter was staring at me.

I flushed so hard my face probably bled through my makeup to match my skirt. He'd caught me practicing.

"I was just…" I whirled my finger in the air, vaguely pointing at my shoes. "I'm not used to heels. So I was just… Never mind. Did you want me to have lunch delivered?"

"No. We'll go out."

"We will? Since when do you go out for lunch?" I swiped at my hair again.

"We don't have that much on our plate today. It's the calm before the storm. We'll go out."

I shrugged and headed back to my desk, knowing he'd also caught that weird seam on my legs that didn't match my outfit. He was the type of guy to notice. My plan to dress to impress swerved a little toward "trying too hard."

I put the thought out of my head. If he hadn't said anything yet, he didn't plan to. And he couldn't get me on the wearing tights thing, because I didn't have a contract on that. Technically, I was in the clear.

The morning passed quickly, as the last two mornings had. It didn't help that Hunter kept interrupting me with his coffee needs, or like last time, his water need. Without Brenda, I forgot all about it. Even still, it felt like he was pinging me every ten minutes.

Or maybe he was, just to see the circus coming through on her new stilts. Doing it with an audience was even worse. If the man ever laughed, or even smiled, I was sure he'd be cracking up at my entrances.

Close to lunchtime, I received an email from the VP of marketing needing a signature. Knowing it needed a quick turnaround, I printed it off immediately and walked it into Hunter's office. He glanced up at my approach, as he normally did today, and then looked at the clock.

"Lunch in about twenty?" I asked as I neared him.

"Yes, that's fine." His gaze hit the paper in my hand.

"This is that document you've been waiting for," I explained as I stopped at the side of his desk and handed it to him.

He dropped it to the surface in front of him and studied its contents, making me realize there was a page number at the bottom, indicating there was more than one page.

"Oh wait," I said quickly, stepping around the desk and leaning over.

He backed up, rolling his chair out of my way as if I had rabies.

"Jeez, not into my perfume?" I muttered absently as I studied the page and then flipped it over. I knew very well I hadn't printed two-sided, and was pretty sure there weren't two pages in the document. I turned it back over, only belatedly realizing it wasn't a one, but a smudge of ink.

"Oh, it's—" I cut off as a warm hand touched my thigh.

My breath hitched as electricity rolled through me.

Frozen, unsure, I waited for what came next. Maybe he was about to move me to the side.

His soft touch traveled up the inside of my leg.

My eyes fluttered closed, and I felt the heat as that palm slid upward. His thumb traced the seam in the tights.

"Oh," I breathed. My sex started to pound. My nipples contracted.

I was in big trouble.

His hand paused for a moment. The roll of his chair filled the space. Another hand, applying firm pressure, touched my other leg.

Walk away, Olivia! Walk away right now!

My fingers dug into the leather of his desk pad. My breath came in fast pants. His hands didn't move as he waited for me to do the right thing. I had the power to enforce our deal. And I should've. I should've straightened up and walked away right then.

But I wanted him so bad.

I could hear his breathing, deep and even. It contrasted mine, fast and shallow.

The pressure of his palms increased, branding my skin with his touch. His thumb stroked, sending ripples of pleasure up my body. I dropped my head, not able to get enough breath. Those condoms were so close. I wanted to feel him push into my body so bad.

"Hunter," I whispered, not knowing what else to say. Losing my grip, and only able to think of his touch. I needed him in a way I couldn't remember needing anyone.

I leaned forward, further onto the desk. I bent, exposing more of myself.

Giving him the permission he was looking for.

Chapter 8

HIS HANDS BEGAN to climb, slowly at first, inching along my stockings until he pushed up, under the skirt. His fingers moved over the edges of the garter. The heat of his touch seared my inner thighs.

"More," I begged, tingling all over.

His hands glided up and over my bare butt cheeks. He lifted the skirt, bunching it at my waist. His palms slid back down to my skin, kneading as his thumbs slipped into my recess. A shift of his position, and suddenly one of those thumbs moved over my swollen sex, covered with the moist lace of my thong.

"Hmm," I said, drooping over the desk with closed eyes.

The chair rolled again as that thumb rubbed. I felt hot lips grace the inside of my thigh right above the tights. His tongue licked up until it traced my panty line. I moaned as he sucked in skin.

His thumb left my skin. I waited, feeling the cool air on the line of moisture from his mouth, so close to where

I needed it. Fingers appeared then, tracing along the edge before dipping under my panties. Material slid aside, exposing my center.

His hands moved my legs further apart before his mouth, hot and wet, covered my folds. The suction coaxed a deep and sultry moan from my throat.

"Oh," I sighed, melting toward the desk.

His tongue tickled my nub in lazy circles, parting my folds and dipping in. He sucked again, running back down my center before landing on, and sucking in, my nub. I rocked into his mouth, feeling his rhythmic suction. Feeling his tongue working me in tandem with his mouth. My panting increased in strength. A long, low moan ripped from my throat.

"Please, Hunter," I begged. My body started to fracture. Cracks started to form. "Please," I whispered, licking my lips.

His rhythmic suction sped up. I gyrated in small movements. My moans grew louder. The pressure in my body so extreme it was almost painful.

The sensations exploded into an orgasm that jolted me forward. I shook against his desk, consumed with the waves of pleasure crashing over me. My body drooped even more as my chest heaved from my labored breathing.

I heard his drawer open. Foil crinkled.

My heart was already beating fast, but now it started to hammer wildly. My body wound up again as I worried about the line I just crossed, and knowing I was about to tap dance over an even bigger one. Expectation short-ened my breath, though. Chased away logic once again. I was swollen and tender, sensitive to the touch. I wanted to feel him inside of me.

A belt jingled. The whisper of pants falling filled the air, followed by the fabric slide of boxers or boxer briefs moving down his muscular legs.

Oh God, this is it. Am I really going to do this?

I knew my answer.

My chest tightened up. I felt like this was my first time: half afraid, half excited. My fingers clutched the desk in anticipation. My breath caught in my throat, waiting.

His blunt tip touched my wetness and slid from one end to the other, and then back again, parting my folds and bracing at my entrance.

I was about to let Hunter Carlisle take what he want-ed. I was about to let him win. He would finally get the girl who said no.

I had no idea if he'd want me on the other side of this. I had no idea if my job would still stand.

He paused just at that moment, probably seeing me tense up. Probably wondering if I wanted to rip away and run for the door again.

I wondered the same thing.

"Tell me," he commanded, his thighs pushed up against mine. "Tell me to fuck you."

I wanted to rock backward, to get some movement, but his hands held my hips possessively. He held the reins of control. He pushed for my submission.

"Tell me," he said again, using that soft command that weakened my resolve.

"Fuck me, Hunter," I whispered.

"That's my girl."

His large manhood pushed into me, stretching me to the point of pain. All the air blasted out of my lungs as sweet glory coursed through my body. The world stopped spinning as he filled me completely and lighted me on fire.

"Yes," I sighed.

He started moving, slowly at first, getting my body used to his size. It didn't take him long to speed up, clearly feeling my urgency. Matching it with his own.

"Yes," I said again.

He jerked my hips back as he bore down. He pulled out almost completely before rocking forward again, knocking me against the desk. Again. My body thudded against the wood. His skin clashed against mine. He pushed faster and harder, hitting all the right places. Dominating me with his powerful thrusts.

"Harder," I begged, wanting him to pound away my presence of mind. Needing him to take me out of myself, like the dress and the lingerie did.

"Do you like it when I fuck you, Olivia?" His voice was deep and velvety. So intense. So consuming.

Pleasure caressed me as he pushed harder. The harsh language contrasted with the silky tone sparked my heat higher. A palm in the middle of my back pushed me down, flat to the desk. He was in complete control.

"Yes," I breathed, the sparks of pleasure turning into scorching bursts in my core.

He hammered into me, rocking the desk. Pounding my body against it. Pinning me with his strength. Working me with his size.

The heat pulsed hotter still, throbbing. "Oh God," I moaned, the tightness unbearable. I couldn't quite get there, though. I was right on the edge, but I couldn't hit that last hurdle. I needed something to push me over. "More," I moaned, straining. Tightening up all over. My toes curled. My hands clutched the desk.

"Hunter," I begged, "Please."

His upper body lowered over mine. His thrusts grew deep and intense. The desk thudded under us, rocking forward on the floor. With his mouth close to my ear, he commanded, "Come with me."

Like flicking a light switch, a wave of raw pleasure hit me. I screamed his name, then God's, then lost the ability to speak altogether, lost in wave after wave of world-ending sensation. I shivered and quaked and moaned under him as he shuddered above me. He moaned in my ear before bending down to lightly kiss my neck.

When I stopped climaxing, he straightened up, pulling me with him. His arms wrapped around me, holding me close for a moment as he trailed light kisses up my neck to just below my ear. Then he whispered, "Always remember, the material things enhanced your beauty, they didn't create it."

He stepped away, and I knew a moment of regret as his body left mine. Taking a slow, quiet moment, only our combined breath ringing in the room, he adjusted my panties and pulled down my skirt. Once done, he put himself to rights, smoothing away all signs of what we'd just done.

He picked up the paper. "Let me check over this document before we go to lunch."

He nudged me to the side with his chair as he sat in it. Then turned away, cutting me off.

I was excused. I could see my way out.

Wow.

If there was a way to feel more cheap and forgettable, I didn't know what it was.

I pulled at the hem of my blouse, then smoothed it out. "I'll just...wait at my desk..."

He didn't acknowledge the sound of my voice.

Wow.

I couldn't help my stiff back as I left the room. Nor could I help the hollow feeling in my gut. I'd been screwed over a time or two in my life, but I'd never felt this...small.

I sat slowly in my chair, staring at nothing. The pleasant ache of my sex reminded me of what I'd just done.

I'd let Hunter Carlisle win.

He'd taken what he wanted, and then he'd dismissed me. I'd let him assume control, and dominance, trusting that he'd take care of me in the process, and he'd done what he always did—fuck and then move on. I had just become like every other admin, contract or not. I let myself be used.

I rubbed at my chest absently. *This hurts.*

As a surge of tears overcame my eyes, I stood and quickly made my way to the bathroom.

This is how he operates, I tried to remind myself. A man who worked with a personal contract didn't put his heart out there. He'd said it wasn't personal. It was business.

It didn't feel like business.

As I stood in front of the mirror, I wiped angrily at my face. Those other women might've been able to do this—they might've been able to shut off, and use him how he was using them—but I couldn't work like that.

I let the pain consume me a moment longer, let two more tears fall, and then tucked it all away and lifted my chin. I took deep, cleansing breaths to calm the sobs.

I had known what might happen with that first touch. I knew when I should've said no, and I'd still said yes. Shame on me. Now I knew what waited through the rabbit hole, and that the best sex of my life wasn't worth the pain and degradation I felt afterward.

The solution was simple: stop giving myself away. If he wouldn't be a decent human being, then he would remain my boss until the month was up, and then he would be the CEO of the company I worked for. The End. Someone else could play the power and dominance games—I was checking out.

HUNTER EMERGED FROM his office a half-hour later with the cloak of business wrapped tightly around him. He walked with his shoulders straight and square, braced to the world. His face, so incredibly handsome, had set in a stone mask with hard eyes.

His bearing, and his movements, suddenly seemed so severe. The cold reserve with which he used to amplify his powerful persona contrasted heavily with the soft touches and passionate embrace from earlier.

And then I saw it. Like standing on the street and looking up at a light flicking on in a dark room, I saw past his harsh exterior to what lay beneath. Finally, I understood. Hunter Carlisle kept the world at arm's reach to safeguard himself. He didn't love, because he didn't want people getting close. He enforced contracts and used harsh language to keep it physical. He was trying to protect himself at the expense of others.

Well bully for him. Whatever his reasons, it didn't make it right.

I assumed my own professional mask. I raised my eyebrows as he approached in a silent question. *What do you want?*

He frowned slightly as he laid the document on my desk. "This looks fine. Go ahead and send it back and then we'll go." He slipped his hands into his pockets.

Hiding the evidence of those digits, eh, bub?

Without a word, I took the page and headed to the

copier to use its scanning feature. When back, and loading it to email, I said, "Brenda put a scanner on order, by the way, so we don't have to waste time walking back and forth from the copier."

"Whatever you need."

I snorted. If a scanner could fix all my problems, I'd be a merry woman, indeed.

Email sent, I reached down for my handbag and moved around the desk to him. I paused, eyebrows raised again, wondering why he wasn't walking forward.

"Have everything?" he asked as he glanced at my computer.

"Yes."

"You won't be coming back. Do you need your computer?"

Startled, I asked, "Am I fired?"

His hard stare blasted into me, his handsome face more severe than I'd ever seen it. "Of course not. But you can finish up Monday. The document I just handed back will give us a couple days of idle time, then I might need you more often. I'd rather give you a break now so you're fresh when I need the longer hours."

"Oh," I said in relief. He was a dick, but I needed the paycheck. "Well, if I don't have to work, then I don't need my laptop. Although…I suppose getting online would still be nice." My phone's screen was cracked and I'd given back Kimberly's computer. I was really glad Hunter had chosen a laptop instead of a desktop for my work computer.

I moved around the desk to close everything up.

"Why don't you have a personal computer?" Hunter asked.

Apparently everyone had wads of cash to buy electronics in his opinion. "It broke." A thought occurred to me. I paused with my laptop half in my computer bag. "This'll work outside of the network, right? It doesn't have any special encryption or anything like that?"

"We're not the CIA, Olivia," Hunter said in a dour voice.

"You think you're important enough to be," I muttered as I returned to my computer. His fabric made a silky sound, indicating he'd shifted. Which also probably meant he'd heard that.

Oops.

I looped the computer case over my shoulder and slung my handbag over my forearm. He started moving as I came around the desk. No words marred the silence. We rode the elevator in silence, too. And then crossed the lobby and walked out onto the sidewalk, all without saying a syllable.

His body moved with a rigidity that implied he realized I wasn't acting with my normal gabby candor. He made no move to question the difference, though. He didn't even glance my way, other than to make sure I was moving through whatever door he was holding open for me.

He either knew our earlier situation bothered me, and didn't care, or just generically knew something was wrong, and didn't care. Either scenario amounted to the same thing. He was an ass. If I had better balance in these heels, I'd be tempted to give him a kick.

We exited the building into the October sunshine with silence pressing against us. One thing was for certain—if we went to lunch like this, I would break down in tears. I needed some time to rebuild my armor.

"I think I'll just head home, if that's okay?" I said as his hand reached out to guide me to the right.

He paused. I angled my face to the ground, unwilling to meet his hard stare.

He said, "I'll have the car brought around."

"No, it's fine." I took a step away. "It's the middle of the day—I can handle it."

"Olivia." The power in his voice dribbled down my spine and sent tingles working back up. Heat spread through my middle and pooled low. I stepped closer to him without meaning to, wanting that heat. Needing his touch again. Wanting his protection even though there was nothing to protect me from except himself.

My biggest mistake had been that first "yes."

"You will take a car home," he continued in a voice that brooked no argument. "There is no need to brave public transportation when you don't have to."

I closed my eyes, hating myself as I nodded. A tear leaked out, making me turn away to hide my face.

"Mr. Ramous—I need the car brought around front. You'll be taking Miss Jonston home," he said into what I presumed was his phone. I couldn't be sure, however, since I was blinking profusely up at the sky in the other direction, letting the crisp air dry my eyes.

A moment later, his voice softened as he said, "Olivia, look at me."

I felt the pull to turn, but resisted. The last thing I needed was for him to see how he'd affected me.

"Olivia—" He cut off as the sleek black car drifted down the street. It stopped in front of us with hazards flashing as Mr. Ramous stepped out in all his bulk.

"I was just down in the alley waitin', sir," Mr. Ramous said as he opened the back door and stood to the side. "Thought you might want a ride to lunch."

Hunter's touch on the small of my back shocked me with electricity, making me jump. I stepped away quickly before walking to the car. Once seated, I took time to carefully stow my bags on the seat next to me so as not to have to look up at those sexy brown eyes. The door closed a moment later, but only when Mr. Ramous sank into his seat and pulled away from the curb did I chance a look out the window.

Hunter stood on the sidewalk, watching the car pull away with his hands in his pockets, a consternated look on his face.

"He can be a hard man to work for," Mr. Ramous said in his barrel-chested rasp. "You never really know what he's thinkin', and he's almost always strait-laced, but once you get used to him, it works out. Some men are all words, making promises and whatnot, but they don't deliver. Mr. Carlisle doesn't do a whole lot of promising. Or talking, even. But he shows you the money. He remembers you on Christmas, and he's generous with buyin' the clothes and things like that. He got my wife a set of earrings last year for our wedding anniversary. He's a good man; you just wouldn't know it unless you hung around a while."

"I don't know how long I'll be hanging around," I said as I watched the city crawl by. Traffic didn't allow cars to get places that much faster than buses. Although the leather seats sure beat plastic, and Mr. Ramous' conversation was much better than that of a stinky man mostly talking to imaginary people.

"Yeah, I was that way in the beginning, too. I mean, the man doesn't even say please, you know what I'm sayin'? Just orders you around. Even the assholes— excuse my language—say please. They don't mean it, but they say it. But like I said, I got used to it."

I could deal with the no "please" or "thank you" situation. I just couldn't deal with the "fuck me, now leave" mentality.

"Well, I'll see out the month and then probably move somewhere else in the company," I said.

"Gotta do what's best for you, that's true." Mr. Ramous' big hands feathered the wheel through his hands as he turned. After a moment, the car slowed to a stop in front of my apartment complex. He slapped the hazard button before rolling out of his seat. This man did not care about parking places—he just stopped where he pleased.

Not that the motorists behind him would say *boo* once they saw his size...

My door opened. "Okay, Miss Jonston." Mr. Ramous held out a hand for the computer bag.

"Oh, no, I'm fine," I said, climbing out of the car.

"Are you sure, Miss Jonston? Wearing high heels is work enough—no sense in carrying things, too. I can take it up for you."

I laughed as tears came to my eyes again, his unexpected kindness contrasting wickedly with Hunter's unfeeling dismissal. Then, once started, I couldn't stop. The pain welled up as I thought of Hunter's disinterested look as he pulled down my skirt. His cold precision as he buckled his pants. And then just turning away, as if I had disappeared from the room. As if I'd just brought him coffee.

I wiped at the tears furiously as a giant arm came around my shoulders. "Ah, don't cry, Miss Jonston." Mr. Ramous pulled me into a bear hug that cracked my back. "Whatever he did, he didn't mean it that way. Trust me, there's been times when I wanted to crack his skull. But he's just closed off—he doesn't know he's doing it. I really believe that. He was raised a certain way. You know those filthy rich types—they are bred without feelings."

My watery laugh muffled into Mr. Ramous' huge chest. "Thanks."

"Nothin' to it." He released me and looked down into my face, concern stealing his expression. "Just gotta get used to him."

"Okay." I sniffed with a smile. "A work in progress. And call me Livy."

He grinned and nodded. "Sure, Livy, but only when the boss isn't around. He has certain ideas about protocol—hence this expensive suit. I sure don't need a suit this expensive, not to drive a car. But hey, he's paying."

"That's what I thought when I bought these clothes." I walked toward the doors of my apartment complex.

"I'm Bert, by the way. Since we're using first names." Bert hurried in front of me and held open the door. "I have your number, so I'll just text you with my driver's line. When you need a ride to work or to get home, you just call me. Mr. Carlisle said I was to watch out for you."

"Thank you." I wiped away another tear at his continued kindness and escaped inside. I needed to come up with a game plan where Hunter was concerned, or I'd never make out the month.

Chapter 9

———∼∼∼———

"KIMBERLY?" I HELD my phone to my ear as I sat on my bed, my work computer out but closed in front of me. Distant voices echoed from Kimberly's phone, as if I was listening to a conversation on the other side of a door.

A moment later, I heard, "Hi, Olivia. Sorry—I was just getting a cup of coffee. So I hear you took the job!"

"Did you hear that from Hunter?" I couldn't keep the accusation from infusing my words.

"No. I heard that from Margaret. She was one of the girls that made it to round two. She works in the company and knows someone in human resources. She doesn't know who you are, or anything, but said the girl Hunter was after ended up signing the contract."

"The standard one," I clarified with a firm voice. "The contract just to be in the company."

"You didn't sign the other one?"

"You can't say anything…"

The phone shifted. "You know I won't! I don't want

Hunter Carlisle as an enemy."

"Well, I have a month to decide about the other one. And that's kind of the reason—"

"Are you *serious*?" she screeched. I flinched, yanking the phone away from my ear. When the high-pitched squeal was gone, I chanced listening in again. "I have *never* heard of him making an exception on that part. Not since he started it. He's really private—I'm blown away. He really wants you. See? Didn't I tell you? You're a diamond in the rough, girl. I can't *wait* to tell that jerk Jonathan who you're working for now. He'll flip. He put in his résumé at that company and didn't hear squat."

"Don't tell Jonathan." I rubbed my eyes. All the emotional stress of the day had me exhausted.

"You're right. It'll be better if he hears from someone else. That'll teach him to just go by appearances. I mean—you know, dress and whatever."

"The reason I called, though," I said hesitantly, "is because I…" I took a deep breath. "I sorta gave in. With the personal thing. Not the contract, but… I just couldn't say no…"

"Oh Lord," she said softly. "He finally got you. Took him long enough. How was it? Was it great?"

My face burned. "Yes," I admitted. "But…after…" Insecurity ate away at me. What if he usually took more time with other girls?

Summoning my courage, because knowledge was important, I hedged. "He was really distant after."

"Oh. Don't worry about that. And don't feel embarrassed, because I talked to a few other girls who made it to round two when I did, and he does that to everyone. He is basically still climaxing when he walks away. I mean, I hardly noticed, because I was still…you know. But he was dressed and back on his computer before I even got off the desk. He was looking over one of my legs to see the screen! Ordinarily that would be really embarrassing to admit, I know, but he does it to everyone. Especially the admin. He never lingers."

I breathed a sigh of relief. It wasn't just me. It didn't forgive his treatment, but it helped with my confidence issues. "He fixed my clothes, but yeah, then he just shut off."

"He fixed your clothes?" Kimberly asked in confusion. "What do you mean?"

"You know…like…put my underwear right and pulled down my skirt. We didn't remove any clothes." I covered my face with my hand. "How are you not embarrassed by this stuff?"

"Huh." Kimberly went quiet for a moment. "He's acting really strange with you. I wonder if he's going through a midlife crisis or something. Or maybe he's worried you'll sue or something. Because, no, he never usually bothers with the other party. His last admin, Jacinta, always said she had to hurry and get out of his way. That's the gig."

I flicked a piece of fluff off my bed. "I'm not into that gig. I wasn't…into that treatment." I hated the tremor in my voice.

Kimberly tsked into the phone. "Oh, sweetie." I could imagine her pouting in response to my distress. "He doesn't mean it. He's just a lone wolf type of guy. A lot of the business guys are like that. He focuses on business, and forgets that people have more emotion than computers. It has nothing to do with you personally."

"It sure felt like it did." I wiped my cheek again and stared at the ceiling. "I think I'm too sensitive for these shenanigans."

"Hmmm," she said, and I knew it was filled with support and commiseration. "It's probably because Jonathan treated you so poorly. I mean, you've had one-night stands, haven't you?"

"Two, and both as a result of crazy parties."

"Well, then?"

"Yeah, but…the mistake was mutual on those. I was sprinting for the door a moment after the guy tried to gnaw his arm off to get it out from under me."

"So what are you going to do?" Kimberly asked softly. "He'd understand if you left, I know he would."

"The money is too good. And plus, I need to do the month to get a job in his company."

"Yeah, my dad was shocked to hear Mr. Carlisle wanted you that bad. He reamed out the head of IT for lowballing you. So, what do you think? Just wear a thick chastity belt for three weeks?"

"Probably." I wiped away more moisture and fell back on my pillow. "I don't really have any other choice."

"Don't look him in the eyes—he can't hypnotize you that way. In fact, just don't look at any part of him. There isn't one thing on that man that isn't geared toward hypnosis."

I laughed despite myself. "I know, he's too gorgeous for real life. Being rich, too—it just isn't fair."

"You'll make it through this, like you do with everything else. And you'll come out on top. You just have to stay the course."

"Yeah." My phone buzzed in my ear. I pulled it away from my face and saw a text from an unknown number that said, "This is Bert. Here is my driver #."

I put the phone back to my ear. "Well, I should go. I have to go grocery shopping if I want to eat tonight."

"A few people are meeting for drinks tomorrow night if you want to go?"

"Jonathan's not going to be there, is he?"

"No. I told Jen not to invite him, since I figured you'd want to get out."

I braced the phone between my shoulder and cheek as I opened up the laptop. "Now that I have a little money to blow?"

"Exactly!"

I laughed as I signed on. "Okay, but just for a little while. I also have a job to get up for, whether I want to or not."

"Yay! Okay, talk tomorrow. And don't stress about this Carlisle thing—you'll get used to him. And when you do, make use of him, because someone that good with his hands shouldn't go to waste."

I scoffed in surprise. "Dark horse!" I accused.

She giggled. "The man brings it out in me, what can I say. Just don't tell Robby."

"As if. Okay, bye."

"Bye."

I dropped the phone to the side as I pulled up my email. I couldn't help myself. I had three, one from the marketing guy blessing me for my promptness, one from the entertainment team talking about a walk-a-thon, and finally one from Hunter I hadn't opened yet.

I let the little white arrow hover over his name, debating whether I would open it. Then, not able to let an email sit idle, I clicked.

From: Hunter Carlisle
To: Olivia Jonston
Subject: Charity Dinner

Olivia—

I've been scheduled for a charity dinner in three weeks' time. You are my plus one. Brenda will add the event to your calendar.

Your dress should be formal and tasteful, but not too conservative. Please choose three contenders and bring them to my office on Monday. Brenda will organize the necessary fittings.

We'll speak more about this next week. Make sure the date and time is open.

H.C.

I hit "reply" and whipped off a quick acknowledgement of having received the email.

Dresses. I didn't get any formal dresses; I'd just bought work attire. I'd have to hit the stores tomorrow, since who knew what time I'd start getting out of work now that I was doing some real tasks.

And those real tasks would *not* include more sex.

As I was clicking on social media, my instant messenger flashed.

Hunter Carlisle: *Why are you working?*

"Why don't you mind your own business?" I asked the message.

Olivia Jonston: *I'm not. Just saw that email and thought I would reply.*

Hunter Carlisle is typing…

I waited, staring at the blue font. The message disappeared, only to flash back up again. Only to disappear again. I rolled my eyes. He was probably doing something else and hadn't realized he was typing in the IM still. I clicked over to the internet, only belatedly realizing I hadn't signed into a VPN, which was what usually allowed someone to get into a secure server.

Olivia Jonston: *Do I not need a VPN?*

Hunter Carlisle: *No. One password signs you in to everything.*

Hunter Carlisle: *Wouldn't someone as technologically proficient as yourself figure that out?*

"You got what you wanted so now you can be a dick, is that it?" I muttered at his name.

> **Olivia Jonston:** Sorry about that. That software isn't widely used due to security issues.
>
> **Hunter Carlisle:** I was joking, Olivia.

"Oh." I tucked a lock of hair behind my ear, wishing I had the courage to type: "I wasn't aware you had a sense of humor."

> **Olivia Jonston:** Ah. My bad. Kay, I'm going to go.
>
> **Hunter Carlisle:** Will you be home in about an hour?

My hands hovered over the keys. I stared at the message suspiciously. Before I could reply, Hunter pinged me again.

> **Hunter Carlisle:** Mr. Ramous will be dropping something off.
>
> **Olivia Jonston:** I should be. I can go grocery shopping later.
>
> **Hunter Carlisle:** I will let him know to make it his priority. He'll text or call when he gets there. Have a nice afternoon.

My hands continued to hover. Two things seemed strange. One, why did Bert have a package for me? What had I forgotten? And two, why was Hunter being cordial over IM when he'd been so standoffish in person?

I wondered if he felt bad. That maybe my reaction had shocked some feelings into him.

"Fat chance." I signed off IM and out of email. I didn't want any more communication from him. Not for the rest of the weekend. My crazy didn't play well with his.

IN AN HOUR I was engrossed in a book on the couch when the door buzzed. Knowing it was Bert, because Jane wasn't home, I bounced off the couch and pushed the intercom button. "Hello?"

"It's me, Bert. I have something for ya."

"I'll be right down."

"I'll bring it up—it's too much for you to carry."

I smiled. "Okay. Level two. I'll wait by the stairs."

"Yes, ma'am."

I pushed the button to admit him. Walking out to the landing, I heard the door close a level down and heard the heavy footsteps of what must be Bert's giant girth plodding up the stairs. I backed up as he reached the top. In his hand was a huge bag with the Apple logo.

"Whatcha got there?" I asked, leading him to the door and then clearing out of the way so he could enter my small apartment.

"I told ya Mr. Carlisle looks after his employees. It appears you need a computer." Bert put the bag on the coffee table. "Mr. Carlisle called in the order. I just picked it up. Open it up, let's see what he got ya."

With a furrowed brow, I walked around him and pulled open the bag. A box displaying the same insignia as the bag looked up at me. Beside it were other, smaller boxes.

I pulled out the large box and gasped at a brand-new MacBook Pro. "He bought me a computer?"

"And what's this?" Bert pulled out a smaller box with a big crater of a smile on his face.

The image of an iPad graced the front of the box.

"And this." Bert pulled out a mouse and additional keyboard next, both Bluetooth, and studied them with a shaking head. "I don't know why he got you another keyboard. You have one with the laptop."

"If I set it up with a monitor, probably," I said as my eyes rounded. "He went crazy."

Bert showed me a new phone, then a pair of head-phones before setting everything down with a smirk. "Mr. Carlisle shows you your value, he doesn't tell you. See what I mean? He's a good guy if you don't let the rudeness bother you."

"In other words, he's a dick, but a generous one."

Bert laughed as he backed toward the door. "You said it, not me." Still chuckling, he kept backing up until he was in the hallway. "Do you need anything else?"

"Like what, a desk to go with all this?"

Bert bowed his head. "Maybe ask him for that next week, Livy. My back is killing me and he'd probably get a solid wood one. I don't fancy carrying it up the stairs."

I laughed and bounded toward the door. "I don't have anywhere to put a desk, don't worry."

"Probably for the best." He started off down the hallway. "See ya Monday."

"Bye."

I shut the door and just leaned against it for a second, staring at the array of equipment littering my coffee table. I could not believe he'd bought all that for me. Without asking, or making a big show of it, he just got everything he thought I would possibly need, and left it at that. If I never said thank you, he probably wouldn't even notice.

"Unreal," I said, starting back over. It didn't heal us, this unexpected generosity, but it certainly made me feel a little less low. A little less insecure. Because no way would any of my ex-boyfriends ever do it, and the last couple had the money to.

I packed it all up with care and moved back to my room like a rat with a rare morsel of fresh cheese. Before I ripped into all the packaging and started playing, I logged on to the work computer and the instant message.

Olivia Jonston: *speechless* Thank you so much!!! I shouldn't accept it.

I waited, staring at the computer. There was no sign he was typing.

I glanced at the clock—a little past four. He'd still be there, I had no doubt. Maybe getting coffee.

I tapped my fingers, glancing over at the big, pretty white bag. I took out the computer again, and then the iPad. I gazed at them with hungry eyes, but didn't open the boxes. I really shouldn't accept them—that had been a true statement. He didn't owe me any of this—he was paying me a wage to work; that was enough. Plus, I had my work computer; I had all I needed.

I pulled my lips to the side as I debated, hearing the familiar *ping*.

> **Hunter Carlisle:** *I got top of the line—I didn't know what you were into. You can exchange what you don't want/need. If you want another brand, let me know and I can get a refund.*

> **Hunter Carlisle:** *And you will accept it. I bet you are staring at it right now, waiting for my go-ahead. Enjoy. I would've gotten you a monitor, but I didn't know your size constraints.*

I squealed in delight.

> **Olivia Jonston:** *This is perfect. Too much. And I don't have anywhere to put a monitor. (I don't have a desk)*

> **Hunter Carlisle:** *We'll amend that when you have more space. Have a good evening.*

> **Olivia Jonston:** *Thank you again!!!*

I didn't wait to see if he was typing. I turned with ravenous fingers and tore into the packaging on everything. I wanted to feel it. I lost the rest of the day to my new devices, and eventually ordered in pizza. Grocery shopping could wait.

"YAY, YOU CAME!" Kimberly sauntered toward me in a cute little red dress with black stockings. Her hair bounced over her shoulder in a tumble of curls. She gave me a firm hug and then dragged me toward everyone else.

They'd chosen an upscale tavern that served oysters and clever creations for nibbles. The floor and tabletops weren't just clean, they were shining in the mid-level light from recessed bulbs. Prices were high, though Kimberly's friends probably didn't notice, and drinks were decent.

Four people congregated in the back around a large, round table. Each already had a drink in front of them with two spots empty. What must've been Kimberly's drink waited in front of one.

"Hi, Livy!" one of the girls, Tera, said with a big grin as I walked up. Her curly hair was pulled back from her face with barrettes. She wasn't usually this excited to see me. Or anyone.

"Hi." I hesitated before sitting down. "Do I need to order a drink at the bar?"

"No, someone comes around." A guy named Jett absently waved toward the bar. The shock of freckles across his nose and cheeks stood out against the pale of his skin.

I sat at the same time Kimberly did. She plunked her phone on the table and sipped her drink.

"I'll just say it—how did you get a job with Hunter Carlisle?" Jen, a girl in her early thirties, asked with shock on her face. She was the oldest in the group, but had graduated at the same time as Kimberly and Jett, having spent some time after high school abroad with various charities.

I glanced at Kimberly and got a slight shake of the head. These people weren't in the know about the personal side of things, thank God.

I shrugged as all eyes found their way to me. "I applied, like I have to a million places, and he didn't kick me out simply because I have zero experience. I'm just an admin, though. I'm not in my field."

"*So?*" Tera exclaimed, leaning forward on the table. "It's Hunter Carlisle! The man is a god in business. I'd do anything to get that position."

"Including him. He is h-o-t!" Jen fanned herself.

Rick, a man with messy brown hair, a full beard, and far more money than sense, rolled his eyes. "Is that why you dumped me? You like pretty guys half your age?"

"He's a couple of years older than you," Jen said. "And I dumped you because you were afraid of the shower."

Rick's even white teeth showed through his mat of beard. "Touché."

The waitress stopped by with a smile and looked at me with eyebrows raised. "Can I get you something?"

"Yes, could I have a mojito, please?" I asked.

"Get her two, and another round for all of us—she's behind," Rick said, making a circle in the air with his pointer finger.

"And a round of tequila!" Tera exclaimed. "Olivia finally has a job—we have to celebrate."

"No way." I waved my hands at the waitress. "No

shots."

"Shots." Tera overrode my complaint with an exaggerated head bob.

"Definitely shots," Kimberly added.

"Whose side are you on?" I demanded of Kimberly.

"Yup, shots." Rick gave a thumbs-up as the waitress moved away.

"It's early, you'll be fine," Kimberly said with an evil grin.

"Now." Tera stared at me across the table. "Tell me everything about Hunter Carlisle. I have been stalking that man forever."

"No, don't, Livy," Jett said as he grabbed a cracker and loaded it with cheese. "Make her sweat."

"It's not like more information would help," Jen said. "Carlisle doesn't make friends."

"I don't need to be his friend, but I'd love to see the inside of his bedroom." Tera's eyes sparkled.

"Can we change the subject, please?" Rick asked with a groan. "This is really putting me off."

MY DRINK CAME and went. The shots came and went. More drinks filled their place. Usually I was able to control my alcohol intake by ordering for myself. Not so this time. When the waitress came around, Rick or Tera took over ordering for everyone, Tera because she thought I should be celebrating the job of the century, and Rick because he didn't do any sort of meaningful job for his father, and mostly just partied. He was ecstatic for any excuse to go wild.

A few times I tried to decline the next round, not because I was concerned about money as I usually was, but because I was on a short ride to Drunk-ville. I didn't drink as often as the others, and didn't have their tolerance. The thing that made me complacent, though, was that for the first time, I was included. I was treated as an insider. I was no longer Kimberly's unfortunate friend that also graduated from their school—I was one of the crowd. It felt good to be accepted for once.

Toward the end of the night, when I should've been sober and asleep, my phone swam into my vision. I blinked one eye closed so I could properly see the numbers, and groaned. After ten o'clock. "I gotta go."

I stepped away from the bar and bumped into Kimberly. She giggled.

"I gotta go," I repeated. "Isss ten o'clock. Too late."

"Oh my *God,* Livia!" Kimberly clamped a hand down on my arm and leaned closer. Her face glanced off my ear. "Ow!" She stumbled backward, rubbing her nose. "Oliv-a." She pointed toward the door.

I swayed as I swung my head too fast. "Why did you make me do shots?" I asked the room in general.

Blurred people, fuzzy and multicolored, tilted in my line of sight. I blinked a couple times and then widened my eyes, hoping that might help my sight.

It didn't.

"What?" I asked, leaning heavily against the bar.

"That *ass*hole is here," Kimberly spat, looking around

wildly. "Where's Rick? Rick'll get rid of him." Kimberly staggered away, leaving me blinking down at my glass of water. I upended the glass in my mouth, belatedly feeling the cold liquid dribble down my chin and onto my chest, soaking one of the blouses I was supposed to reserve for work.

"Least it's just water," I said, swaying backward as I tried to look down at my chest. I groped for the bar and pulled myself back in. "I gotta go. Bad idea. This was a bad idea."

"Olivia." The voice tickled me in places I remembered vividly.

Chapter 10

—∾—

I SWAYED TOWARD him, quickly caught in his arms. I glanced up into the face of Jonathan, the ex who tore my heart out and broke it apart like a wishbone.

"What're you doing here?" With water dribbled all down my front, and my makeup probably all over my face, I wasn't showing him what he was missing.

He showered me with that smile I remembered so fondly, fluttering a deep well of emotion.

"I loved you," I blurted, falling into his embrace. "Why did you do...that-to-me." With my finger I made a motion like a spinning turbine. "Pre-tend I...am talking-at-normal speed."

His carefree laugh made me sigh. Those handsome features captured me. I'd stared at his face for hours, making love, cuddling, and laughing. We had our hard times, but on average, he'd made me happy.

"Why're you here?" I leaned forward and braced my forehead on his chest.

"Because I heard you were here, and thought you

needed a ride home. Or would you rather go to my place?" He tilted my face up and leaned down until his lips glanced off mine. "I thought maybe we could start things up again. I shouldn't have let you go."

"Oh no, bro?" Rick stepped up beside us. I felt his hand grab my upper arm and pull me away. "What happened to Crystal?"

"This doesn't concern you, *bro*," Jonathan said in icy tones.

Kimberly put an arm around my shoulders, staring at Jonathan. "You didn't give a *shit* before she got a job with Carlisle." Kimberly jabbed a finger at him. "You're just trying to use her, you heartless *bastard.*"

"Oh, spare me." Jonathan's gaze came to rest on mine. "Why don't I take you home. We can talk."

"I gotta go," I muttered, shrugging out of Kimberly's grip and ambling away.

"Wait—" Jonathan started.

"Don't even think about it," Rick said.

"What are you going to do, bro?" I heard, but I wasn't turning around to watch a male pissing contest. I had to get out of there.

I stumbled outside. The chill of the night draped around me. The temperature revived me a little, but soon it would make me shiver.

I lurched to a stop and made a U-turn. The closed door stared at me. If it could, it would've quirked an eyebrow, I was sure. "Are you sure you want to go through here?" it would ask.

And it had a point. Jonathan was through there. "He'll seduce me." That was bad.

I brought up my phone, which had stayed clutched in my hand somehow, and felt the weight of my handbag on my other arm. I glanced down to make sure, staggering forward with the shift in weight.

Yes, that was my handbag.

"Lucky," I announced. A couple passing by glanced at me. I staggered backward to get out of the way.

The bus was out of the question. I was in bad shape. Very dangerous.

"Cab." *Stop announcing things out loud!*

I brought my phone up again and closed an eye, willing the image to solidify into one object. The glow of the screen made me squint as I brought up my contacts list and tried to scroll with a clumsy finger.

I hated this, being drunk. Buzzed was one thing. Even bent toward inebriated I could handle. But fullblown incoherence was no fun.

Too late now.

The screen lit up with a name. "Oh shit." I stabbed at the red rectangle and missed. The image changed again—call connected. I couldn't hang up now or I'd be a crank caller.

"Hello?" I asked as the phone neared my ear.

"Olivia?"

I leaned against the wall. "Yeah—sorry. Didn't mean call you." I pulled the phone away and squinted at the screen again, making out a blurry "Bert" as the title name.

"Oh shit—sorry, Bert! You don't even know me and I'm an asshole. Sorry! Accident." Someone else came out of the bar. I shuffled further over, regardless if it was helpful or not. "'Kay, bye."

"Do you need a ride?" I heard.

"No, 'm good. Under control, Bert my man. Under control. See ya!" I pulled the phone away and stabbed again, this time ending the call.

"Well, that was embarrassing." I winced again. "*Shhh!* God, I am drunk."

"Let me take you home."

I meant to groan, but I think I moaned instead. I closed my eyes as the familiar hand wrapped around my middle. Familiar lips, warm and soft, tickled my neck before landing on my lips. I fell into the kiss—literally. Off balance and out of my head, I threw an arm around his shoulders and face-dived into him. His tongue entered my mouth and I let it, wanting to feel how I had felt with him in the height of my happiness. Wanting that safety and comfort again, especially with all the turmoil I was going through at work.

"I'll take you home, Livy." I let him half lead, half carry me down the sidewalk. My phone vibrated in my hand. I tried to see who it was, but it was trapped in the hand around Jonathan's shoulders. He looked at the screen as it neared his eyes before I gave up trying to see and slumped back against him.

"Is that Hunter Carlisle? Do you know any other

Hunters?" Jonathan asked as he slowed. He stepped to the right and braced me against the wall with his shoulder as he tugged the phone out of my hand.

"No! I need to hold on to that, or I will lose it."

"Hello, sir, this is—"

I bent forward to see that Jonathan had taken the call.

"No, hang up, that's *my boss*!" I reached for the phone, but Jonathan pushed my hand away and half turned to cut me off.

"No, sir, she's right here. I was just going to take her home—she's had a bit too much to drink."

"Way too much," I groaned. "Tell him non't worry. *Don't* worry—I'm taking a cab."

"Jonathan Banks, sir. I recently graduated from... Hello?" Jonathan pulled the phone away from his head. The wallpaper showed, which meant Hunter had hung up on him.

I chuckled. "He doesn't like it when you kiss his butt."

"He has your direct line, huh?" Jonathan asked, looping a hand around my waist and helping me up.

"Obviously." I leaned on Jonathan. "Phone, please."

Jonathan must not have heard me, because he continued to hold the device as we ambled down the street.

"Are we close?" I was regretting not getting that cab. I wasn't up for the long walk in the cold with these heels. Quality heels were still heels, and there was a breaking-in period that wasn't kind on my feet.

"Just up—"

A motor revved in the street. The glare of red signaled a stopping car. Bright yellow hazards flashed before Jonathan stopped, turning us toward the street. A man approached, wide shoulders decked in an expensive suit. He didn't stop in front of us. Instead, he stepped to my side, put an arm around my back and one under my legs, before sweeping me up.

"Whoa," I said as his strong arms squeezed me into his chest.

"Is that her phone?" Hunter asked, staring down at a wide-eyed Jonathan.

"Yes," I answered as my head lolled against Hunter's shoulder. "'S okay. He was taking me home. Put me down, Hunter."

Hunter's hold didn't relent.

"I was just giving her a ride, sir. You didn't need to—"

"Did you not think to offer her your jacket?" Hunter demanded. "She's freezing."

"S'okay," I murmured, my face comfortably nestled against the heat of his neck.

"Well, sir, we were almost to my car, so—"

"Give me the phone," Hunter interrupted in that commanding voice.

"Of course, sir."

Hunter shifted and we were moving, walking between two parked cars and to the side of a sleek gray sports car. I had no idea what kind. Nor did I care. It was a ride, and right now, that was all I really wanted.

"Can you stand?" Hunter spoke quietly in my ear. His voice was soft, reminiscent of the time we were intimate.

"Mhm," I said against his skin with my eyes closed, relishing his warmth.

I felt movement until my feet gently bumped concrete. I let him straighten me up, keeping a hand on me while he shrugged out of his suit jacket.

"It's fine. I don't need it, Hunter, honest." The chattering of my teeth gave me away, though.

"Here." His jacket draped over my shoulders, wrapping me in his delicious scent. I snuggled in, handing him my handbag so I could put it on properly. He opened the door and handed me inside then shut it behind me.

The heater blasted my face and the warmth of his jacket radiated around me. I sighed in contentment as I leaned into the luxurious leather, realizing belatedly that Hunter was taking a long time to get in. Glancing around, I noticed him back on the sidewalk, talking to Jonathan. With his straight posture, I couldn't tell what message he was delivering, but with Jonathan hunching within Hunter's stare, it couldn't be good. After a moment, Jonathan nodded adamantly. Hunter stalked toward the car and then sat in the driver's side.

"What're you doing here?" I sounded like a broken record, despite the fact that he was not the person I had originally asked that question to.

"Mr. Ramous had some concerns about your well-being."

"Why'd he call you?"

"He wanted to know if he was overstepping his bounds to go get you. I said yes, since you weren't on company time."

"Yet here you are."

"I don't have the same constraints."

I closed my eyes as his expensive machine purred to life. "I was trying to call a cab. Don't know how Bert came up."

"And your ex-boyfriend?"

I furrowed my brow at the vicious tone in his voice. When I glanced at his face, though, illuminated by the red of the dash, it was completely impassive. I closed my eyes again. "He offered me a ride. I really did love him, once."

"Not now?"

I directed my gaze out the window. "I dunno. A little, I guess. When he kissed me I remembered the happiness. But I'm hurt, too. And I know better. Usually."

"Dare I ask why the copious amounts of alcohol?"

"Do you ever just do stupid things to feel included for once?" I chuckled to myself. "Pro'bly not. You show up and you're the hit of the show. And look, you were my ticket in. 'Cause of you, they like me. Go figure."

"They like your connections. Now you're connected to money, status, and power. They were raised to think that is important above all else."

"Not Kimmy! She's not like all that."

Hunter clicked a button on his dash. "No, she is mostly good stock. Her father is a good man, if a bit eccentric. But she keeps those friends all the same. You are a beloved pet project—at least you started that way. I have no doubt she's seen you as a friend for a while, but she just hasn't matured enough to realize that your type of friendship is much more genuine than those around her."

"Says the man who's the same age as she is. So what makes you an expert? You live in the same social circles."

He was quiet for a moment as he pulled to a stop in front of my apartment complex. "I belong to a similar social class, but I don't exist in the same circles. My life is work. Business is cold and unfeeling and it always makes sense. It always has made sense. That's enough for me."

"Are you sure?"

The question lingered in the silence. After a while, I peeked an eye open. He sat back in his seat with his gaze rooted to my face. His clenched jaw and hard eyes gave him that severe look. I recognized that look as trying to push distance between himself and others. Me, in this instance.

"Is this the part where I assume your silence means get outta here?" I fumbled with the seatbelt.

A blast of cold indicated Hunter exiting the car. I hit the button. The seatbelt whizzed from around me as my door opened. I took his hand, feeling the electricity crawl up my arm and heat my body before settling deep into my core.

"Oh no, not now." I squeezed my eyes shut as he pulled me from the car. I didn't want to see what was in those sexy bedroom eyes, nor did I want to look on that impeccably handsome face. Both of those things would add fuel to the already blazing arousal coursing through my body.

"Jacket." I started to pull off the jacket when my legs were swept out from under me. I squealed, clutching muscular shoulders as Hunter clasped me to his chest.

"Bring it to me tomorrow."

"I can make it from here."

I know he heard me, because I said it right next to his ear, but he didn't slow. Neither did I. I slid my arms around his neck as I licked the edge of his earlobe. Warnings were absent, hidden in the alcoholic numbness. Bad decision-making was a green light, despite what I'd been thinking not ten seconds before.

I sucked on his neck below his ear, giving him a small bite. I heard his hard exhale in the silence of the stairwell.

"Put me down here, Hunter, and kiss me."

The man was good at ignoring me.

Undeterred, I sucked harder, knowing I'd leave a mark, wondering if he would stop me. Or speak. He did neither. Instead, he stopped by my door and said, "This one, right?"

"Yes, stalker."

He set me down in front of the door and leaned his body into me. I felt his hard bulge in my stomach, and for a moment, when he bent, I thought he would take me. His hands reached low. I hooked a leg around his to give him more access.

Instead, my keys jingled as he took them out of my purse.

"Seriously?" I flung an arm around his shoulders as he bent to pick me up again. "You'll seduce me in your office, but not in a fun place like a stairwell?"

"Where's your room?" he asked in a strained voice.

I pointed before my lips went back to nibbling his hot skin. My fingers trailed down the middle of his chest, popping buttons as I did so. By the time he closed my door, I had the button against his belt line undone and my hand pulling out the bottom of his undershirt.

"Stop," he whispered.

I didn't.

My feet lightly bumped the floor as my hand ducked into his shirt and met bumpy muscle. I straightened up as he did, so I could reach up higher, feeling over a rock-hard pec. "When do you find time to work out?" I murmured, exploring with my palm.

"Where are your pajamas?"

"Don't need them." I pulled out the rest of his shirt as he stripped the jacket from me. He tossed it on the end of the bed before pulling my blouse over my head. I leaned my head back, pulling on the back of his neck.

"I can't, Olivia." The words came out strangled.

"Yes. You can. You do it all the time." I undid his belt, pulled down his zipper, and then reached in and grabbed the velvety skin of his shaft.

His hands covered mine and gently removed them before re-securing his pants. I stared up at him in hurt confusion. "You were fine with this yesterday, but now, suddenly you don't want it? It's because I do, right? You don't like not calling the shots?"

He turned to my bed and pulled back the sheets. "You don't want this, Olivia. It's the alcohol talking. To give in would make you hate me for it in the morning. I don't want to see the expression tomorrow that I saw yesterday."

I shifted, resting a hand against his perfectly sculpted six-pack to show I was still brazen, but my eyes filled with tears. "I didn't have an expression," I lied.

"You think I don't know what glassy eyes and a dejected look mean? It's been a long time since I was involved with someone, but I remember what it looks like when I trample on a trusting soul. I should give you up, I know I should. That's the right thing to do. But I can't. I want you, but not like this. Not when you aren't in control. Only cowards and hustlers prey upon the weak and confused."

I dropped my hand and head at the same time. "I just can't win with you."

"I wish you wouldn't try."

"Please, Hunter." A tear dripped down my face as I looked up. "I don't want to be rejected. I don't want to be cast aside, not tonight. Jonathan made me feel... I just don't want to be alone. I'll remember I pushed myself on you, and while I might regret it, at least it was my choice."

His thumb came up and wiped my tear away. "And when you wake up alone tomorrow, after we...have sex? Then how will you feel? I can't stay, so even if I give in, you'll wake up alone and know that I left shortly after. It'll be worse than me leaving now."

Another tear rolled down my cheek, but this time an angry one. "Fine. Leave, then."

I pushed him out of the way, discarded the rest of my clothes, and slipped into bed. I tried to suppress a sob as my face dripped with tears. I heard a sigh before the bed compressed next to me. A hand settled on my upper arm. "Look, I'll compromise, okay?"

I didn't respond. I didn't see how we could compromise—not with his track record. Nor with mine.

I heard fabric rustling before pressure on my arm had me rolling to my back. He sat without his shirt, exposing the most glorious chest and arms I'd ever seen. Cut pecs led down to deliciously bumpy abs. His arms bulged and his lats were cut from stone. My mouth dried up with need so great I couldn't think straight.

"I'll pleasure you until you say when. Then I'll leave." His fingertips traced a line of fire down my chest. "You call the shots this time. And when you're sated and asleep, I'll go."

"Your car?"

"I doubt anyone is going to call me in at this time of night on a Sunday, but I can easily get a ride from the car service you never use."

"Must be nice to have money out your ears."

"Not always." He bent down to my nipple. A hot dart of pleasure shot down to my core as he took it into his mouth. I moaned as his other hand traced my other nipple.

"Take your clothes off," I said, running my hands up and over his shoulders. The suction increased, rolling my eyes into the back of my head. "Please."

His mouth lifted right before the jingle of a belt sounded. Fabric slid on skin. He crawled onto the bed, pushing my knees apart with his hands. A warm, wet tongue started at my clit and moved in lazy circles before dipping into my folds. He tickled me at first, light and teasing, making me squirm. His mouth went back, sucking while his fingers dipped into my body.

"Hmmm." I ran my fingers through his hair as I arched back, jutting my breasts into the air with the sensation. He sucked harder, his fingers moving in and out in rhythmic thrusts. Cold shivers raked me, flowing down my skin. Bursts of heat fired within my core. Hot and cold, shivering and tingling, his fingers worked, faster and faster. His mouth sucked and his tongue swirled, playing me like an instrument.

I moaned loudly, straining into his mouth. Yanking his hair. Feeling my body start to vibrate.

"Hmm, Hunter," I moaned, thrusting my hips.

He worked faster, plunging his digits as his mouth never let up. My body wound tight. My breath came in hoarse pants. And then I blasted apart, moaning with the release as I quivered.

His mouth dipped lower, lightly sucking at my inner thighs before moving back up and barely glancing across my hips. He sat up for a moment, looking down on me. With the light from the window, I could see his gaze linger on my breasts, travel down my stomach before lingering on the vee of my legs, before connecting with my eyes. "You're beautiful."

I sat up slowly, wanting to kiss him so badly it hurt. As I wrapped my fingers around his neck and pulled him toward me gently, angling my mouth up to him, I saw a flash of fear in his eyes. Wariness took over, and I knew he wouldn't. Whatever the reason, it was internal, and kissing was a no-fly zone.

Instead, I bent to his neck before kissing down his chest. His breathing became louder, less controlled. I circled his navel with my tongue before grabbing his hips and pulling upward. He rose up to a kneeling position. As he did so, his large cock, fully erect, came closer.

This was supposed to be about me. But I wanted to taste him. I wanted to hear his release of breath as he gave in to the feeling.

I licked the tip, hearing him suck in a breath. Gently, teasing him as he had me, I lightly skimmed the surface with my tongue. His hands came away from his sides. I grabbed the base and sucked in as much as I could handle, gagging with its length.

"Ohhh." His fingers worked through my hair. "You shouldn't, Olivia—"

I backed off as I stroked with my hand, hearing that exhale. I sucked in again, massaging his balls, before starting a slow rhythm.

"That's not part of the deal," he whispered in a voice filled with pleasure. "Ohhh," he sighed again, his hand tightening my hair.

Excited shivers started in my gut as he started to direct my effort, taking control. I sucked greedily as I stroked, working in harmony, building him higher.

"Oh God, Olivia, you should stop."

His face tilted down toward me. His gaze connected with mine, and I saw a new spark of pleasure. He watched me as I worked, moaning softly as I took him deeper than I ever had any other man. His thrusts got bigger and his moans more pronounced.

"Ohhh, Olivia," he whispered. "I'm going to come."

I didn't pull away, letting him empty into my mouth as he flexed his body over me. I stared up at him, at his magnificence, strong and powerful. I ran my hands up his sides as I straightened back up. His palm came to my jaw and his other hand lightly cupped a breast. For a moment, all he did was look into my eyes, quietly. Softly.

This was the Hunter from the day before. The man under the armor.

Unable to help myself, I traced the edges of his lips

with my fingertips. I leaned forward slowly, seeing that fear resurface. It immediately subsided as he realized where my lips were aimed. I kissed his cheek softly, pulling him close until he put his arms around me. My lips traveled up his jaw line until I was simply hugging him, feeling his body against mine.

In his velvety voice, with the command riding the words, he said, "Lie down. I want to feel your body."

I fell back into the sheets. His palm ran from my knee up, over my breast and to the base of my neck. He lay down next to me. His face was inches from mine. Our breath mingled. His hand kneaded my breast as he leaned forward and kissed my chin. Softly, his kisses worked up my jaw. I ran my leg up the outside of his thigh, sighing when he rolled a bit, covering part of me with his warm body.

His kneading became more intense as my swollen sex started to throb. His knee came up, moving my thigh high on his hip. His lips dragged across my jaw to the edge of my lips. They touched down as his hips swung upward. I felt his blunt tip poke my wetness.

I gave a soft moan. My hand slipped to his chin, lining up his face with mine. I looked into his eyes, feeling the tension mount. Feeling that tip right at my entrance. Wanting him with everything I had.

"Do you want me to fuck you, Olivia?" he said in his deceptively soft voice.

I moaned as his power licked up my body. In a breathy whisper, I replied, "Yes."

He rolled onto me. His tip prodded, pressure right at my opening. His eyes scanned my face as he made soft thrusts. His tip pushed, widening me. Preparing me for entry, but not engaging.

I dug my fingers into his back as I arched, needing more. Needing him to fill me up. "I have a condom in my drawer," I whispered.

"I want to feel you. You're still on the pill?"

"Yes."

His palms slid along my arms and pushed my hands above my head. I could feel him shaking over me. "Lord help me, I can't say no to this, Olivia."

He gave one hard *thrust.* I moaned, falling into that exquisite pleasure. As my hips rose, trying to get him deeper, my body tightened up, nothing in the world better than his hard length searing inside me. There was just him and me and the friction between us.

His eyes hit my lips. A flash of longing stole his features as he picked up the pace, pushing into me with heady thrusts. He lowered, kissing my cheek and my jaw, my neck—everything but my lips.

The pace picked up. My legs and arms tightened around him, the sensations overwhelming me. "Yes, Hunter!" My eyes fluttered as my body wound up, his ends hitting off mine.

I turned my face until my lips glanced off his. I gave a light kiss to the corner of his mouth.

He groaned. His thrusts became manic. Desperate. He entwined his fingers within mine. "Give in to me,

Olivia. I need you."

"Yes, Hunter," I moaned, letting go just that little bit more. Opening up to the sensations.

He labored, pounding into me, forcing out moan after endless moan as my core tightened. "Please, Hunter," I said, unable to take the sharp pleasure any longer. Needing release. Striving for the end.

"I need more of you, Olivia," he said in a low voice, rising up so he could work harder. He pulled my knees higher, at his waist now, and bore down. His large cock dove deeper, hitting new sensations. Driving me higher.

"No," I said, fingers digging into his shoulders. Nails bit flesh. "No, please," I begged, feeling the tension tug at me. The emotion he was pulling out sucking from deep inside of me.

He pushed harder, his delicious body shiny with moisture. Mine sleek and slippery. My legs wrapped around his middle as my body hit a new high. I gasped in ecstasy.

He ran his hand down my chest, stopping on my breast. He pinched a nipple, making me moan in delight.

The bed was squeaking now, keeping our pace. I groaned with each thrust at my end. My core was so tight. My body so sensitive.

"God, you feel so good. I don't want this to end." Hunter laid his whole body on me, his movements deep and forceful. The demand in his movements unmistakable.

I felt a little more of me erode away. I gave just that

bit more, unable to help it. Wanting him to take me all the way.

And then he said, "Come with me, baby."

With two last, hard thrusts, I screamed out my orgasm. My whole body quaked with the exquisite release. Hunter shook over me, groaning into my neck. My body convulsed, milking his release.

As we calmed down, he rose up on his elbows and looked down on me. His eyes were so open. He bent and softly kissed the middle of my forehead.

"That felt good," I said as my eyes drifted closed.

He chuckled softly. "I have a suspicion my car has gone."

"Sorry," I whispered. "I'd offer to pay, but you have more money than me."

He rolled me to my side and snuggled in behind me. "I took advantage after my big speech about being better than that. And in your room, no less."

"Better than the stairwell—we would've had peepers with how loud you made me scream."

I felt his light kiss on my neck. "I'll stay for a while longer, but then I have to go."

"I know," I said softly, sleep tugging on me. "This was my doing. I'll deal with it in the morning. You're blameless. I pulled out the tears. That's never fair."

"Listen, Olivia, tomorrow, when you wake, remember that I'm as screwed up as they come. I'm incapable of things normal people find so easy. These faults are mine—they have no bearing on you. If I was a better man, I wouldn't chase you. I would accept 'no' and leave you to your life in peace. But something in you calls me, and I can't walk away. I want you too much. There is a special place in hell for people like me. You'll move on from this one day, and you'll see that nothing I did was a reflection on you, except for my inability to walk away. I'm sorry—for this…for everything. Please remember all that tomorrow."

My eyes drifted closed as the words filtered in, but I didn't take much meaning in them. Before I knew it, I let sleep tug me down into the abyss with his heat wrapped around me.

Chapter 11

I WALKED IN to work the next day not knowing what to think. Hunter had saved me from a bit of a pickle. He'd stopped whatever he was doing to rip me out of Jonathan's greedy clutches. Jonathan was a mistake I did not need to make. Thanks to Hunter, I hadn't.

Cue next mistake—I'd all but forced myself on Hunter. He hadn't wanted to have sex with me, but I'd pushed him into it. By crying. To a man, that was like slipping him a drug.

I ran my hand across my face as I waited for the elevator. I had wanted to stay away from Hunter sexually. Instead, I had pounced on the guy.

I jabbed the "up" button a few more times. *What is taking this thing so long?*

The man waiting beside me took a step away.

Hunter was being a good guy last night. He'd not only felt bad for Saturday, something he probably wasn't used to doing, he then tried to make it up to me by doing the right thing. That failing, since I was hanging off him like a groupie, he'd tried to compromise. The man was a saint last night, no two ways about it.

I marched into the elevator in a cloud of frustration. There were so many facets to this issue.

My mind recalled his look of raw fear every time he thought I might kiss him. It wasn't my breath—something had happened to him once upon a time, and he had an issue with that form of intimacy. Real intimacy. He could shut off with the physical stuff, like a hooker, but with kissing, something tugged at him.

I slammed my index finger into the floor button. The person who'd gotten in behind me shifted uncomfortably.

Why had I gone and confused this situation even more?

I felt the ghost of his body moving against me, entering me in a haze of passion. My body heated up and a wave of perspiration broke out across my forehead. I started fanning myself in the elevator.

Ah, yes. That was why. The man was a god in bed. A. *God!* The way he touched me, and how he moved—there weren't one in a million like him.

I wanted to do it again. Right or wrong, I wanted him with a fervor I didn't understand and couldn't control. Right now, next to a nerdy man with a comb-over, I was having an arousal hot flash to rival all hot flashes across the globe. My sex was swollen and my nipples were so hard they threatened to cut through my bra. I wanted to march into Hunter's office and rip his clothes off.

"Oh Lord, I'm in trouble." I started fanning myself harder.

"What was that?" the man asked. I could hear the uncomfortable tremor in his voice. He thought I was crazy.

He was right. Hunter made me this way.

The memory of Hunter's words as I was drifting to sleep resurfaced. My chest tightened up with emotion.

He thought he was fucked up. He knew what he had done to me Saturday, he was worried he'd do it again, and he hated it. He hadn't rejected me that first time, he'd protected himself. Like he always did. He shut off and dove back into business. The two were incredibly different.

I'd landed myself in some mess. I really had. Because I didn't want just sex from Hunter, and I definitely didn't want to walk away. I wanted to get to know him. I wanted to know why he thought he was fucked up, why he was afraid of intimacy, and the big one...if he could love. Because I could love. I knew I could. And I worried with all that was in me that I could very easily love him. Last night had clenched it.

I turned to the man in the elevator. "I am in a world of trouble, my friend. Bear witness."

His eyes widened. He clutched his lunch bag to his chest but didn't speak. A moment later, the elevator chimed and he hustled from the confined space.

Hunter really was making me crazy.

When I hit my floor, I slunk into my desk area, looking around with shifty eyes. I wasn't sure how I would handle Hunter yet. He'd be shut off, and I was worried it would hurt me. In this case, logic and emotion were completely at war.

"Olivia, are we going to have a problem?"

I froze with my handbag halfway to the drawer.

Brenda stalked toward me with a scowl and two cups of coffee. She put one cup on the desk and then balled her fist and jammed it into her hip.

I stopped my hand from jerking toward the red welts Hunter had left on my neck last night. My high-necked sweater should've been covering them. Calling attention to his love bites would announce my guilty conscience.

I continued lowering my bag into the drawer, nice and slow. As I straightened, I used a light, musical voice as I said, "What's that, now?"

It was clear that espionage would not be a career option for me.

"You know that I review the credit card transactions, right?" she asked.

"Yes…"

Brenda pursed her lips. "And are you not under strict orders to take the car service, or a cab, instead of the bus?"

The exhale left my lungs in a *whoosh*. Thank God—she wasn't onto me. "Yes, but I was running late today and didn't have time to wait for the car."

"Mr. Ramous was waiting for your call. When he

didn't get it, he called Mr. Carlisle. Mr. Carlisle then had to call me and ask that I check up on your spending habits. I do not like getting a call from Mr. Carlisle on my personal line. It really ruins my morning. I swear, Olivia, you are the only person I have to scold for *not* spending."

"It's so stupid. Cabs are way more dangerous—I mean, I'd essentially be alone with a strange man. The bus has crazies, yes, but there are always plenty of witnesses."

Brenda smirked and moved toward her desk. "Just...make him happy, would you? Then he won't have to hound me and cause a panic attack that I killed a multimillion-dollar deal by not seeing an email or something."

"Okay, okay." I pushed the power button on my computer as I remembered his coffee. A wave of butterflies rolled through my stomach as I started toward his office. Despite myself, I really wanted to see him. In fact, I kind of wanted to sit in front of his desk, with my chin on my hand, and stare.

"Oh, and I saw that you charged a large purchase yesterday at Wilshire—"

"Oh *crap*!" I stopped and turned back to Brenda. "Those were the dresses. I forgot to bring them in today."

"Yes, I wondered, because you're not wearing anything new. But I should let you know... Well, I'll let him tell you." She went back to her computer.

Oh sure, good call—add explosives to the cauldron of crazy I was stirring.

I took a deep breath and walked into Hunter's office. He sat at his desk, showered in light from the bright windows behind him. His suit jacket was removed, showing his muscular shoulders through his light blue button-up shirt. I noticed the hint of pec, which I knew led down into a divine six-pack. I gazed at his handsome face as I drew near.

I set the cup down on the corner of his desk with a shaking hand. He looked up and immediately those bedroom eyes sucked me in, moving something deep in my chest. Something that wasn't sexual.

"Hey," I said in a release of breath. I pushed my hair out of my face, trying to play it cool.

His gaze took me in for a moment, expressionless. Then he said, "Brenda sent me details of your spending. She then furnished me with your receipts. Like all my admins, your spending will have to be monitored. Unlike my other admins, you aren't spending *enough*. We'll be going shopping together at noon today."

My stomach flip-flopped. I didn't care about shopping, but I was all for spending more time with him. "I forgot to bring the dresses."

His gaze snagged on the side of my neck where the bites must've peeked above my sweater. His eyes flashed with hunger. He clenched his jaw and clasped his hands on the desk, turning his eyes downward.

He was fighting his desire. So was I. I hoped he was

better at it than I was.

Or do I…?

I would punch myself right now if I acted on my lust. I would!

"You only bought the three dresses, I take it?" he asked, his voice hard.

"Well…" I adjusted the sweater. "Yeah. I mean…how many dresses does a girl need?"

"Olivia—" His nostrils flared in anger. He turned back to his computer. "Noon."

AT NOON, HUNTER appeared at my desk with hard eyes and a set jaw. "Let's go."

I finished typing an email message, hit "send," and grabbed my handbag. "Okey-dokey."

"The jewelry is coming this evening, as requested, sir." Brenda didn't even look up as she delivered the message.

"Good. Do you need lunch?"

She did look up then. "When will you be back?"

Hunter gave me an assessing stare. His eyes traveled the length of my body, bringing a blush to my cheeks as heat pooled in my core. "We'll probably be a couple hours."

Brenda glanced at her watch. "No thank you, sir. I'll be famished. I'll get something in a while."

He started walking to the elevator, not acknowledging her answer. I lurched to a start, following. I gave Brenda a wave she didn't notice and met him as the elevator was opening.

As we walked through the lobby a moment later, I couldn't help it. I had to satisfy my curiosity. "Was your car still there?"

He opened the glass door and guided me through with his hand on my lower back. Bert waited at the curb with the driver's side, rear door open. Hunter didn't answer me, just walked to the other side of the car and slid into the front seat.

As I approached Bert, I said in a low voice, "Sorry about calling you! I was trying to call a cab."

He glanced at Hunter getting into the car before whispering, "Sorry about calling him." Bert jerked his head toward Hunter. "But I didn't want to just turn up."

"No, it's fine." I waved Bert's concern away. "He got me out of a tight spot, actually. An ex-boyfriend turned up. I wasn't making great decisions about then."

"I can tell." Bert winked as he tapped his neck. He thought Jonathan had given me those, not Hunter.

As the heat colored my face, I slipped into the car. No way was I going to set the record straight.

A short time later, Hunter and I walked into a store I hadn't been to before. A saleslady strolled in our direction. As soon as her gaze hit Hunter, a flash of recognition widened her eyes. A smile spread across her face. "Hello, Mr. Carlisle! Lovely to see you."

"We'll need to see your cocktail dress options, and a couple of business wear items," Hunter answered in a bored voice.

"Of course." Her gaze shifted to me, quickly giving my outfit a once-over. "Anything for you?" she asked Hunter.

"No, not today."

"Great." The lady turned to the side and extended her hand toward the back of the store. "Right this way."

As we walked, the woman fell in beside Hunter instead of me. "What are you thinking for her? She has a great figure—I think accenting her bust and hips would be best."

"Yes. Something low cut, to accent the gracefulness of her neck, and either something short or with a slit, to show the definition in her legs."

"Oh yes, she has great legs," the woman cooed.

I crossed my arms. I felt like a prized pig being dressed up for the county fair.

"Can I get you anything?" the lady asked, bending at the waist and smiling widely. She almost seemed like a stewardess. "Water, tea…"

Hunter looked at me. "I'm fine," I answered politely. He shook his head at the woman.

"Okay, then." She straightened up, smile still in place. "Go ahead and take a seat. I'll just grab some things and see what we think."

When she was gone, Hunter crossed his ankle over his knee before saying, "My car was still there, yes. I was surprised."

I tapped my knees with my fingers. "I don't have any regrets, just so you know. You're in the clear." It was a small lie, but he deserved it.

"No, I'm not. Not by a long shot. But there's nothing we can do about it now."

"Actually, there is. You can let me take credit for last night and stop being a know-it-all."

His head jerked toward me but I ignored him. I just wasn't in the mood today. My head was pounding.

"Okay, shall we try some things on?" The saleslady gave me a beaming smile. If Hunter had planned to say something, he'd missed his opportunity.

Thus began the dress-shopping marathon. Hunter looked at me with an analytical eye, noticing the cut, the style, the way it fit, and the fabric. He vetoed things for the smallest of reasons, like a wrinkle just under the breast. At one point I offered to stuff my bra, just to move on. That would be a terrible solution, if his scowl was anything to go by.

The saleslady, animated at all times, brought me an endless stream of dress after dress. Red, blue, purple, striped, plain—she offered them all. Some were so atrocious I shook my head before I even grabbed the hanger. Horizontal stripes would do me no favors—I didn't need to try the thing on to prove it! Unfortunately, I didn't have the power of veto like Hunter did. He still made me try it, only to prove me right with a head shake.

"Told you," I'd mutter.

Occasionally, when he really liked one, he'd tell me, "Slow down, Olivia, let me see." His eyes would burn with pleasure, or desire. In response, my body would heat up, and make my movements more sensual.

"Turn around again," he might say, his voice deepening.

My breath would get dense. My core would tingle in anticipation.

And then he'd say yea or nay and send me back to the dressing room.

After the third dress I had just turned off. What was the point? If he didn't plan to rip the dress off and drag me into the dressing room, I was just getting worked up for nothing. And that was tiring.

After two hours and what must've been fifty dresses, I was miserable. I would rather have gone to the office and given myself paper cuts.

"How about this one?" The saleslady gave me that annoyingly bright smile as she held out a dress. She still looked fresh and vibrant, probably hearing the ding of the cash register with each dress she handed me.

"Try it." Hunter sipped an espresso.

"Why even ask?" I said to the saleslady as I grabbed the dress. "You know he'll tell me to put it on." I shot Hunter a surly look. This was now beyond ridiculous. I doubted there were any dresses left in the store I hadn't tried.

"You'd be in heaven if this was *Pretty Woman*." Hunter smirked at me.

"Real life versus a movie. How strange that they should be different." My tone dripped with sarcasm. I trudged toward the dressing room. "I didn't know silk could chafe."

"You'll thank me when this is all over." Hunter sounded downright tickled.

I sighed loud enough for him to hear. It was a passive-aggressive "Screw you!" I stepped into the dress and brought it up before flicking the curtain to let the saleslady know I needed a zip-up.

"Oh, now *this* one is fabulous!" She adjusted the way it clung to my body. "Yes, this is simply amazing. I almost didn't grab it—it's a size too big. We've barely been able to keep it on the shelves. But they run small, so I took a chance."

"Great," I said in a dry tone. "Do me a favor: don't take any more chances."

"There are always other stores, Olivia," Hunter called.

Yes, he was definitely enjoying how much I hated this.

I walked out of the dressing room with unfocused eyes and gave him the usual robotic turn.

"Slow down, Olivia, let me see." I heard porcelain clink as Hunter put his mug onto the saucer.

I slowed my twirl, careful not to hunch, lest he tell me to straighten up and turn again.

"No, Olivia, I want you to move naturally in it." Something in his tone had changed. It was subtle—I couldn't quite place the difference.

I followed his instructions, feeling a strange tingle as

he stood. "Come here," he said softly.

The hush of his voice made my hairs stand on end. Suddenly, as I walked to him, I felt silky and sexy and more feminine than I ever had in my life. I took his hand as I stopped right in front of him, only half a foot between our bodies.

"We'll take this one," he said to the saleslady. His eyes drifted to my lips. "And the others I put aside. Put them on my account. I'll be up to sign in a moment."

"Of course, sir." She smiled at me and made herself scarce.

Hunter ran his hand over the swell of my hip and up. When he got to my bust, his hand dipped around my back and applied pressure, making me step closer still. His breath dusted my face as he looked down on me. His other hand slid under my palm and turned over, holding and then raising my hand. He clasped it to his chest as he stepped toward me, forcing me to step back.

A ghost of a smile brushed his lips. "I see you now, dressed like this, and I see nothing but pure elegance. I wouldn't look twice at you if I were seeing you for the first time. I would assume you'd been around money all your life, and your pursuits were entirely material." He stepped to the side, making me, once again, step with him. "Put your hand on my shoulder, Olivia."

I did as he said, stepping forward as he stepped back, slowly dancing in a clothing store to no music. To Hunter, it didn't seem to matter.

"But I met you when you were wearing old clothes

and carrying nothing but hope, and your achievements on a piece of paper. You weren't concerned with the natural beauty you radiate so effortlessly. You showed off your accolades and your intelligence. You gave me something to admire. To wonder about. I pair that woman with this woman, and know you will fit anywhere you choose. And at the end of this month, I want you to choose this job. I want you to choose me."

Chapter 12

BRENDA LEFT AT six that night, as usual. Before she said farewell, though, she led a short, balding man with two large briefcases into Hunter's office. When she came back out, she gave me a salute. "Have fun getting dressed like a doll. And thank God it ain't me."

I watched her walk toward the elevators with a furrowed brow. Ten minutes later, Hunter pinged me.

Hunter Carlisle: *Come in here.*

"Please," I finished for him, dropping my pen and hopping up.

I walked through the door and found the two men at the round table on the other side of the room. The briefcases were open at the edge, their contents sparkling in the failing light from the windows. Hunter sat at one of the seats, looking at the table, and the man stood beside his briefcases, watching me walk closer.

As I neared, I saw what was laid out on squares of black velvet across the table. My step slowed and my mouth dropped open. "What is all that?"

Hunter glanced up. "The dinner is a formal affair and you are expected to represent this office. We have your dress, and now we need to accent it. Go put the dress on so we can see it on a live model. It's in the restroom."

My gaze hopped from one piece of velvet to the next. Sparkling diamonds, some paired with rubies or sapphires, or other gems. Tennis bracelets, rings, earrings, necklaces—there was even a brooch or two. If ever there was a time for sticky fingers and a life of crime, this was it.

"Don't they usually have stores for this kind of thing?" I asked, drifting toward the bathroom.

"Mr. Porter is aware that he will make more money if he comes to me," Hunter replied. "Now, hurry—I have some things that need my attention."

"Please," I muttered.

After I had the dress on, I took a seat next to Hunter, staring at all the sparkling gems in front of me. The sun was already disappearing behind the other tall buildings in the downtown area, showing the room in sharp lines from shadows. Mr. Porter, the balding man, set up some lights near the table so that we could better see the twinkling riches in front of us.

"What catches your eye?" Hunter looked at my chest in a concentrated squint before perusing the options on the table.

I looked from one necklace to the other. I pointed at

one with a diamond at the point and three smaller diamonds to either side leading up into a V. Mr. Porter walked around the table immediately, picked up the necklace, and fitted it around my neck.

"Too small." Hunter looked back at the table. "As it stands, the eye hopelessly dips to her cleavage. I'd rather give people another attraction to admire."

"You picked out the dress," I said under my breath, placing my hand on said cleavage.

"I agree completely," Mr. Porter replied, putting back the necklace.

Of course he agreed. Bigger meant more money.

"Might I suggest a diamond and ruby choker?" Mr. Porter moved to his briefcase.

Hunter watched as the necklace was fastened to my neck. Mr. Porter pulled my hair away from my face and piled it atop my head.

I took a mirror from the table and held it in front of me. The large diamonds and rubies winked at me in the light, swirling around my neck in a light show. The dress, a deep crimson that closely matched the rubies, hugged my breasts just right. There was something missing, though.

I put my hand to my chest right below the middle of the choker. "It would be better with a little something dangling here, wouldn't it?"

"Turn to me," Hunter said.

I did so as Mr. Porter adjusted his arm so my hair was still on top of my head, but his body was closer to

Hunter so he could see. He nodded slowly as Hunter analyzed.

Hunter said, "Yes, I agree. Mr. Porter?"

"Let me see what I have." Mr. Porter dropped my hair and moved to his briefcase. "Would you prefer a ruby, diamond, or combination of the two?"

"What if it wasn't a choker, but just a necklace that hugged the neck before dangling down toward the breasts?" I traced the path I meant, drawing Hunter's gaze.

"That might look better," Mr. Porter said.

"Let's see both." Hunter's gaze drifted to the side of my neck again, snagging on his handiwork. I flushed, drawing his eyes to mine. A deep surge of hunger flared, intensifying his gaze. My body matched, falling into those entrancing eyes.

"Here we are." Mr. Porter came around us again, ending the moment. He dangled a large oval ruby surrounded by diamonds from the choker.

"That particular style doesn't work with that dress, but possibly something along those lines," Hunter said.

Mr. Porter went back to his briefcase and pulled out something with a smile. "I think I have just the thing!"

He fitted the new specimen to my neck and draped my hair around my face. Immediately Hunter said, "Perfect."

I held the mirror up and gasped. The design work was beautiful. Small and medium-sized diamonds looped and condensed, like bows, along the sides of my neck

172

until the loops became bigger and more dynamic where the rubies were worked within the swirls of the diamonds. It fell down my chest in a stylish, intricate design, almost like lacework, the gems just off center in a way that made it unique and different. The size of the whole piece said "Power accessory," but the lacy design said "Elegant." It matched perfectly with the dress.

"A tennis bracelet for the wrist, I think," Hunter said. "And simple diamond studs for the earrings. The necklace will be the centerpiece."

"Refined, sir, as always. That piece is one of a kind. We are sampling the works from a new jewelry designer." Mr. Porter busied himself finding what Hunter asked for. He fitted me with a couple of bracelet options and held up earrings, but I couldn't stop looking at the necklace. I absolutely loved it. It was artistic and refined, as Mr. Porter said, but flashy as well. It made a subtle statement in a bold sort of way. If it were made out of silver and fake gems, I'd love it just as much as the real deal, because it was the style that made it exquisite.

"You like it?" Hunter asked in a quiet voice.

I smiled with supreme joy. It was the joy from *feeling* pretty. It didn't matter how the world received me, I *felt* like a million bucks. I hadn't felt this good in a long, long time.

"Yes, I really do," I said, touching the necklace gently. "When I was a little girl, I would dress up in my mom's clothes and jewelry for when my dad came to pick me up. I'd pretend he was the driver, and I was being taken to an awards ceremony, or a luncheon with famous people. He'd knock on the door in this old suit jacket and black hat, pretending with me. I just…felt so glamorous, you know? This necklace, and the dress and everything, gives me that illusion."

I traced the necklace with a delicate finger, admiring it in the mirror. My eyes glimmered with unshed tears as I thought of my dad. Thinking of the fun we used to have.

"How long can you borrow it?" I asked.

Hunter turned to Mr. Porter, who was standing idle near his briefcases. "We'll take them."

"Of course, sir." Mr. Porter began packing things away.

I stared at myself for a while longer before deciding I needed a bigger viewing area. I wanted to have the image stored away in my mental banks. I could bore grandkids with the memory in my golden years.

I went to the bathroom in the corner of Hunter's office and stared at myself in the full-length mirror. The light caught the gems and threw the light, making me glitter and shine with each movement. I slid my hands down my waist to where the dress cinched, creating that hourglass figure I'd admired on other women. If I had white gloves, I'd expect Prince Charming to knock on the door at any moment, ready to load me into a coach.

I moved back into the room like I was entering a ball, grinning like a fool.

Hunter stood at the window, facing out. He turned

when I glided back in and stared at me for a moment. I couldn't see his expression with the shadows falling around his face, but his body language said he was in one of his closed-off moods. He'd probably be gruff and mean in an effort to fool the world into thinking he was a cold, heartless bastard.

I didn't care. I was floating on air.

"I feel like a Disney princess," I said as I walked over to Mr. Porter. "I definitely need some heels, but look at me!" I twirled with a giggle.

Mr. Porter smiled with me. "Yes, you do look a vision."

I breathed out a smiling sigh as I held out my wrist. "De-throne me, good sir. Even Cinderella has to be wary of midnight."

"It's not what you have on the outside that glitters in light, it's what you have on the inside that shines in the dark," Hunter said from across the room, staring out the window.

"Well quoted, sir." Mr. Porter tucked the bracelet into a pouch and left it in the middle of the table. He did the same with the other items, each getting their own bags. When he was finished, he straightened up and grabbed the handles of the briefcases. "How will we be treating this transaction, sir?"

"Purchase. You have the account."

"Very good, sir. Would you like boxes, then?"

"Send them to the office. That'll be all."

"Yes, sir."

I watched Mr. Porter walk from the room with his briefcases, feeling an uncomfortable clench in my rear. "Purchase?"

Hunter turned from the window and moved toward the table. "Yes. They suit you. I think you should have them."

My heart beat wildly. A cold sweat broke out over my body. I started backing away from the table. "No. No, no. No way, Hunter. Those things are worth a fortune! I'll wear them to the dinner, and I'll let you buy me the clothes, but the jewelry is too much. And this isn't like with the computer where I really do want them and hope you don't make me return them—this is a hard no. Do you hear how high my voice has gotten? That's panic high."

"Your eyes shine brighter than the diamonds when you put that necklace on. That's worth the price." His voice was so soft as he came to stand in front of me. His eyes so deep and genuine.

"No. It sure isn't," I said as tears came to my eyes. No one had ever said anything that sweet to me. "Don't be endearing right now, Hunter, please. That purchase is making me extremely uncomfortable."

"Which is why I trust you will take good care of it." His eyes trained on my lips as his hand came up. He traced the edge of my jaw.

An electric surge lit up my body. Goosebumps spread over my skin. Heat flared, consuming me. I remembered the feel of his body from last night. The look in his eyes.

He was looking at me the exact same way now. Soft and deep.

I ran my palm along his chest, wanting his touch.

He shook his head minutely. That was it, though. His refusal was shallow at best.

Bad idea, good idea, I figured I'd just go with it.

I stepped closer, running my other hand up as well.

His smoldering eyes took me in. I could see the uncertainty warring with desire. I knew he wanted this just as badly as I did. I also knew he wasn't used to someone else calling the shots. He was trying to learn his lesson from last night.

I'd tried that once. It ended a moment ago when I realized I needed him with a raw force I couldn't hope to understand. Didn't want to.

I let my hands slide down his torso and then over his hips. I stepped just a little closer until our chests were almost touching. I cupped his rock-hard bulge. He was ready for me. He could be as uncertain as he wanted to be, but this had to happen.

I rubbed with one hand, threw the other over his shoulder, and stood up on tiptoes so I could trace his stubble with my lips. He still hadn't moved. Hadn't given in to my advance.

I had to play dirty.

Continuing to rub, feeling his body flex against me in arousal, I gave him a small lick and kiss to the very corner of his mouth.

The dam broke. He grabbed me by the back of the

neck and pulled me forward, tight against him. He bent to kiss my neck as his arms reached around. The *zzzz* announced my zipper being pulled down. A moment later, he had slowed long enough to delicately remove the dress and drape it across a chair before stepping back. His hands roamed down my body before slipping into my panties.

My breath hitched. I clutched his shoulders as one of his digits felt my wetness. It dipped into my body.

"Hmm," I said as my fingers flew down his front, undoing buttons. I ripped his shirt open before spreading my hands up his torso.

His hand started to work faster as his mouth nibbled on my earlobe.

I undid his belt and yanked it out of the way. I worked at his trousers, hearing his breathing speed up to match mine. I undid his button and unzipped before reaching in quickly and capturing his smooth shaft. I slid my hand along the velvety skin as I angled my head up, wanting his mouth on mine. As I glanced his cheek, heading for gold, he bent. Two thumbs hooked on the straps of my panties and pulled them down.

When he stood back up, I dropped my arms around his shoulders and hooked a leg around his waist, giving him access. He didn't even hesitate to take it. With a hand on the base of his shaft, and one around my back, he ran his tip along my wet slit. I felt him at my opening, nudging. He grabbed the back of my knee, hoisted my leg up a bit higher, and rocked his hips upward.

"Oh God." My eyes fluttered. The world stood still for a moment.

He grabbed my butt and picked me up. I swung my other leg around his waist, squeezing him with my thighs. I gyrated, feeling the delicious friction as his manhood moved within me.

He groaned as he walked me to the table and set me down. My butt bumped off the cool surface before he leaned down on me, lowering me onto the wood. His lips found my neck as his hips pumped, coaxing a long moan from my throat.

I clutched his broad back as he thrust again, hard and passionate. I squeezed, gyrating up as he bore down, and took him deep. Unable and unwilling to focus on anything but his body inside mine.

"Hunter." I panted. His skin slapped off mine, his cock inside me, rubbing just right. "Yes, Hunter!"

Awareness fled. Control followed. I held on for dear life as he pounded into me, his breathing just as ragged and labored as my own. The table screeched across the floor. The chair holding the dress fell over. His flexed chest rubbed against my sensitive nipples.

"Almost," I said through clenched teeth, straining. With each thrust the sensations intensified. His cock hammered into me, deliciously hard. I climbed, at the edge, just about there.

Tense, flexed, my head dropped back as he gave another hard thrust.

"Oh!" I blasted apart. Pleasure crashed through me. I

quivered, scraping my nails down his back in ecstasy.

He groaned a moment later with his lips near my ears. He snaked his hands under me and around, holding me tightly in his strong arms as he shuddered. He dug his face into my neck, giving a last few thrusts as he finished inside me.

The room was silent except for our breathing. I was still wrapped tightly in his arms despite the awkwardness of the hard table. Panting, I just lay there for a moment, hoping the table didn't break under our weight.

After a moment, longer than when he'd taken me on his desk, he unraveled himself and straightened up. Without a word, he stared down at me for a moment, his gaze as soft as before we started. Bottomless.

He took my hands and pulled me up to standing. "Do you need help putting on your clothes?"

I smiled sheepishly, glancing down at my panties. "No, I think I can manage."

He looked at me for a moment longer, his expression blank. "I'll hold on to the jewelry for now. I trust you don't have a safe?" He raised his brows as he fastened his pants and started working on his shirt.

"No. I barely have any gold, let alone diamonds. My mom kept all the family heirlooms my grandmother tried to pass down."

He nodded like he'd thought as much. It didn't take a genius, after all. He'd seen my room.

Hunter turned toward his desk.

I stood for a moment, wanting to argue about the

purchase and wanting to coax more conversation out of him. But he'd shut off again. He sat down at his large desk and turned toward his big screen, ruling his empire with an iron fist and exceptional business sense. I no longer registered as a presence.

My gaze drifted back to the table. I could barely feel the uncomfortable clenching at the innocent-looking packages in black velvet. Nor the uncertainty over how he could just shut off. Not in the aftermath of that glorious climax, and how long he took to disconnect this time around.

Was he starting to open up just a bit? Was he letting down his guard enough to enjoy being with someone, even for just a little while?

I had no idea, and there was no way I was asking. Instead, I shook my head at the craziness of the evening and walked toward the bathroom to get dressed. I needed to stop trying to do the right thing. It was more fun being bad.

THE NEXT FEW weeks went by in a blur. The charity dinner turned out to be an excuse for the leaders of various organizations to get together and talk business while also donating large amounts of money they would then use as a tax write-off. Hunter planned to approach the CEO of a smaller, and mostly limping, company with a possible plan to buy out.

Brenda was nearly pulling her hair out with the arrangements and scheduling, since this was an out-oftown affair, but I was doing okay. I hadn't been out of college long enough to forget times of intense stress. Having been a member of several clubs and groups, as well as taking a large load of classes, I was pretty used to having no life.

Time passing meant a looming deadline for me. The charity dinner was tomorrow, and a few days after that lay my deadline. I had to choose if I would stay or go.

On one hand, I was having the time of my life. I learned something every day. I was picking up on how Hunter handled business, manipulating and pulling strings at will, and how Brenda organized and balanced the workload of a major CEO. The job was challenging, rewarding, and great for my career.

On the other hand, there was Hunter. I hadn't made an advance since the day in his office, but Lord how I wanted to. Every time I was near him I felt surges of electricity. I wanted to touch him, or lean into him, or just stare.

I could tell he was suffering from the same affliction. When I put a hand on his arm, or he touched the small of my back to direct me, his body would flex and his jaw would clench, and he'd stare at me with raging heat infusing his eyes.

Neither of us made a move. We were ungodly busy with something extremely important to him. He rarely had the business mindset turned off, and I refused to be with him if he didn't. This was put to the test a couple times when he pinged me.

Hunter Carlisle: *Come in here. Remove your panties. I need to fuck you.*

A zing of excitement had gone through me. And, like the douche I was, I couldn't help myself. I walked into his office with a fluid body. When I got in there, though, he stood robotically, undid his belt, took out his manhood, and stroked it to life as he continued to look at his computer.

"Actually, I don't have time to get you wet. Get under the desk and give me a blow job." He'd motioned toward the floor.

I hadn't known what to say. I just stood there, mouth open and rigid.

His eyes met mine. For the first time I could ever remember, he flushed.

He had forgotten it was me at the admin desk. I could've been a stranger for all he cared. He just wanted to stick his dick in something warm and wet.

It was a wake-up call.

Completely embarrassed, I'd turned around and gone back to my desk. Emotion welled up in me, that old feeling of being used. Oh how I hated it. It turned my heat to ice. It turned my eyes into aqueducts.

"I apologize," he had said later that night. "I…wasn't thinking."

"It's fine. Don't worry about it."

"Olivia…" He'd stared down at me for a time. Neither of us spoke. Then he'd put his hand in his pocket and walked toward the elevator. I had no idea where he was going, nor did I ask.

He'd done it one other time. When tensions were high and report due dates were looming, he'd sent me another sexual ping.

Hunter Carlisle: Come in here. Take your top/dress and panties off. I need to fuck.

Olivia Jonston: Come out here. Bring flowers and chocolates. Prepare to recite Shakespeare. I need to laugh.

Nothing had happened. He hadn't responded.

Olivia Jonston: FYI. That was a no.

Hunter Carlisle is typing…

No message came.

Olivia Jonston: Pop quiz, hotshot. What am I wearing today?

Hunter Carlisle: Pink blouse, black skirt with a small slit up the back, black shoes of terrible quality that still give you blisters, hair with no product, and no makeup.

Hunter Carlisle: I apologize about my ping. I was on autopilot again.

Olivia Jonston: I feel sorry for your future girlfriend. You'll cheat on her without any recollection of doing so.

Hunter Carlisle: Impossible. I won't have a girlfriend.

I'd rolled my eyes and gone back to work, stupidly flattered that he'd paid so much attention to me even though, at the same time, he'd forgotten I was there entirely. Most guys wouldn't notice an outfit. As busy as we were, the fact that he noticed I came to work was amazing, let alone that he paid enough attention to notice the Band-Aids on my heels from where the shoes rubbed.

A moment later I got another ping.

Hunter Carlisle: *Regarding the fuck, though... Still a no?*

I'd blurted out laughter. Brenda looked over with a quirk in her brow.

Olivia Jonston: *I never did get those flowers and chocolates. Or the Shakespeare. So...tit for tat. I'm waiting for my tit.*

Hunter Carlisle: *You have great tits. I'd love to tease them.*

Olivia Jonston: *I need my tat, then.*

Hunter Carlisle: *I can give you a white tramp stamp. Come in here to collect.*

"Jesus Christ."

"What?" Brenda looked over.

"Nothing." I didn't fancy telling her that her boss was extremely horny at the moment. And that was making me extremely horny.

Hunter Carlisle: *Did I go too far? I wasn't serious. Mostly.*

Olivia Jonston: *No, but...you're a bit wound up.*

Hunter Carlisle: Yes. This is my sole outlet. And you're beautiful. Yet I am forced into abstinence.

Hunter Carlisle: FYI. I will settle for pity sex.

I had contained the laughter that time. Brenda would want to be in on the joke and I didn't feel like explaining.

Olivia Jonston: No time. I have to get some reports out. Too bad.

Hunter Carlisle: Yes. It is. I apologize again.

Olivia Jonston: No worries.

I'd wanted to keep up the banter, but I had a million things to do and it was already late.

He hadn't slipped up again. He had also kept his distance.

Then there was the contract. It was like a black cloud directly over a picnic. I kept looking up at it as I ate my sandwich, wondering when it would ruin my day.

I'd talked to Kimberly about it, and she said I could try to get around signing it, but it was unlikely. Hunter liked things laid out and squared away—I was a huge loose end.

She was absolutely right.

The evening before the dinner, I sat at my desk staring at the computer, thinking about that contract and what I might be able to change to make things more reasonable. I didn't notice the powerful stride of my boss until he was suddenly right in front of me.

"Oh. Ah, hi." I shuffled papers in front of me, belatedly trying to look busy.

"Why are you still here?"

I glanced at my computer. The time read 8:53 p.m. "Crap. Where'd the time go?"

"Do you have everything for tomorrow?"

I ran my fingers through my hair. "I think so. Everything you requested is done. It's just a day trip, so I don't need much."

He stared down at me for a moment before dropping a folder on my desk. "I've revised a few things. I figured I'd give you a couple days to look it over and ask any questions."

I realized what was in the folder. "Is this negotiable?"

"Signing the contract? No. Not if you want to work in this role. I work a certain way, and I need my admin to support me in that. I like her role clearly defined."

"What about my needs?"

"You have a social life to fulfill your needs."

My heart dropped. He knew very well I didn't have much of a social life. "So, you get to list all the things that would make your life perfect, and what do I get?"

He paused for a moment. "You get access to me."

Angry tears surfaced. "Black and white, huh?"

"Olivia, that's how I work. You know that. I need the chaos contained."

I tossed up my hands. "Well, I just don't know if I can sign something like this. I don't know if I can give away my freedom."

"I'm not throwing you in a jail cell, Olivia. Nothing would change."

"Except for you being able to tell me when and how often I am to fuck you." I wiped a tear from my face as I stood.

"You didn't have a problem with that the last time we were together."

"I was calling the shots the last time. I didn't get a summons to walk into your room, fall to my knees, and blow you."

Hunter's eyes darkened. "Are you saying you wouldn't like that?"

His words pierced me. Unexpectedly, my core tingled. Playing dominance games was hot. I ignored the fantasy, though. "It's not about the sexual act, it's about the collar you want to put around my neck. It's about the leash you want to hold."

"It wouldn't be like that."

"Oh?" I stuffed my computer into its bag and slammed a drawer closed. I brushed hair out of my face and grabbed my handbag. I stared at him defiantly. "And how would you know? When did someone make *you* sign a contract like that? As I recall, your admin can't ask anything of you. She just has to do as she's told. Like a dog."

I snatched up the contact and stuffed it into a pocket of my computer bag. "I'll be ready by one o'clock tomorrow afternoon. I'll be out front of my apartment, so text if you're going to be late."

"Mr. Ramous is waiting downstairs to take you home."

"Mr. Ramous can shove that car up your ass, for all I care. I'm taking the bus, and you can just fuck off."

I stormed out of the area and stood in a temper waiting for the elevators. If he came to stand with me and insist on taking me home, I had planned to berate him loudly all the way through the lobby. He hated calling attention to himself, and since I was slightly hysterical at the moment, I wouldn't mind making a scene.

He didn't approach, though. If he stood and stared, or went back into his dungeon, I couldn't say. I kept my eyes straight ahead, and when the elevator chimed, I walked in without a sideways glance.

I didn't even know what things Hunter had changed. He might've very well calmed down the things that I had an issue with. But the problem with misplaced tempers was that they weren't rational, and often, they had to run their course.

When I stepped onto the sidewalk a few moments later, I saw Bert waiting for me, the door open.

"Not today, Bert," I said, passing by. "See you tomorrow."

"Livy, please let me take you home. Mr. Carlisle won't be pleased…"

"I'm counting on it, Bert. Kiss the wife for me." I kept walking like a woman with a purpose.

I didn't know if I planned to say no to Hunter yet— I'd read the contract, check his revisions, and weigh the implications. Maybe he really was leveling things out. Maybe he was thinking with fairness in mind.

I scoffed at my own thought. And maybe he was a spoiled little brat that always got what he wanted. Because if that was the case, he was just about to learn what "no" felt like. I'd found my courage to stand my ground again, and I would use it.

Chapter 13

THE DOOR BUZZER sounded at ten a.m. the next morning. I cinched my robe around me as I pushed the intercom button. "Hello?"

"Miss Jonston, it's Pat—I'll be doing your hair and makeup, and helping prepare."

"Come on up." I pushed the button to let her into the building.

I opened the door and stood in the doorway. A tall, sophisticated woman in black slacks and shirt crested the stairwell. She had enough luggage to travel to Europe for a week. She turned my way without prompting. When she neared, she asked, "Are you showered?"

"Yes, I'm all set. Aren't we a little early—" I cut off as Bert stomped up a moment later with another couple of bags. "Jeez. You have more?"

"Women prepare for an event in style, Miss Jonston." Pat waltzed into my apartment. "We do not *get ready*. We pamper. Please, let's get started."

Bert stopped in front of me with a concerned look.

"You okay?"

I shrugged. "Meh."

He grinned. "Whatever you got going with Mr. Carlisle, you sure had him surly yesterday. He left right after you did, saw me standing there, and gave me that *look*. You have some balls, girl—excuse the language."

"It's only a job, Bert. A great job, with great benefits, but if you let yourself get pushed around, who are you then?"

"His bitch. You're right." Bert laughed and motioned me through the door ahead of him. "I don't think he's used to it."

"Rich people rarely are, are they?"

Pat was setting up in the living room. Makeup of all kinds and shades spread across the coffee table. Hair products and tools littered the couch. A chair from the kitchen table had been brought over and was waiting for me to sit.

Pat straightened and looked me over as Bert headed toward the dining table in the corner.

"Can I clear some of this off, Livy?" Bert asked as he set bags down.

"Yes, go ahead. We'll just have to put it back, because it's my roommate's. And I wouldn't leave the car too long—DPT are pretty fierce with issuing tickets during normal working hours."

"Mr. Carlisle said he wants to enhance your natural beauty, not overshadow it." Pat gazed down at her tools and colors. "He was absolutely right. Bert, bring up the dress, if you please."

"Yes, ma'am." Bert put down a bottle of champagne he was about to open and headed for the door. "I just have to grab it from the car."

"He's so helpful," Pat mused as she glanced at my face again. "So much sweeter than the last driver. I hope he stays for a while."

"How long have you worked for Mr. Carlisle?" I asked as Pat picked out a couple shades of concealer.

"Oh, I don't. No offense, but I would never work directly for that man. His moods would drive me insane. I have my own shop. I usually wouldn't do house calls myself—I have girls for this kind of thing—but saying no to Mr. Carlisle is not wise if you want to keep his business. And I would certainly like to do that."

"Here we are," Bert said as he returned. "I'll just leave it here. I saw a space open up across the street. I want to go grab it so I can sit in on the fun."

Pat waved him away as she turned to the dress. She took it out of the garment bag like she might an old relic, before hanging it on a picture frame in the middle of a white wall. She tsked. "My, my, that is something. Absolutely gorgeous. You have great taste."

"I was just the model. Hunter picked everything out."

"Ah. Well, he chose well for you." She sucked her lip as she surveyed her makeup options again. "My instinct would be to use bold colors. To really play up the glamour of the dress and make your eyes pop. Hmm."

She crossed her arms and spun around, looking at the ground. "Where are the accessories?"

"I don't know. Hunter was keeping them."

"Yes…" She crossed to the table and bent for a small black box. As she brought it over, I realized it was a strongbox. "Locked."

Pat laid it on the couch. "Well, we'll have a mimosa while we wait for Bert. No sense in standing around idly."

We were halfway through our glasses when Bert trudged into the room with a sheen of sweat on his face. He huffed as he closed the door. "Had to fight someone for the spot. I got there first, but he tried to nosedive in. Sneaky little…"

"I hope you didn't have to get physical with him, Mr. Ramous." Pat winked at me. "Your opponent would be a pancake."

"No, but I did have to get out of the car when he started yelling." Bert walked over and grabbed a bottle of water. "He didn't stick around long. I got to pull in."

"I bet he didn't," I muttered with a smile.

"Okay, Bert, if you will, please unveil the jewelry." Pat pushed away from the counter in the kitchen and showed Bert the box she'd moved.

Bert bent over the couch to retrieve it, entered a code, and pulled open the container. He handed it to Pat.

"Mr. Carlisle doesn't even need a strongbox—just put the merchandise on Bert's person somewhere, and he'd be all set." Pat's eyes twinkled as she smiled at Bert.

"Ah, now," Bert said with a red face. He grabbed a chair from the table and set it near the door. It was removed from the battle zone of hair and makeup, but still a part of the crew, given the tiny size of the apartment.

"O-kay!" Pat's eyes lit up as she pulled out the bracelet. "This is nice. Classy, yet simple."

She opened the next velvet bag and delicately pulled out the contents. "Oh my God!" She gently held the necklace in her hands. "He wants you done up to the nines. Lucky girl."

"Wow, Livy," Bert said, standing and stepping closer to get a better look. He glanced at the dress, and then back again. "Saying no really does the trick. I've never seen him go that big for an admin before."

"He can probably see that *this* admin isn't after his material possessions," Pat said, draping the necklace over my chest. Her eyes darted between the necklace and my face.

"I didn't know he was going to buy it. I tried to stop him," I exclaimed. I picked at my nail, suddenly extremely uncomfortable.

Pat froze.

"He bought those?" Bert asked with incredulity.

"Don't pick your nail—you'll make my job harder." Pat unfroze as the moment passed. She put the jewelry away carefully. "And don't be so alarmed, Bert. Obviously he sees something in this girl that he hasn't seen in the others. Hell, *I* see something in this girl that I never saw in the others, and I've known her for five minutes." She gave me a wink. "Don't feel uncomfortable—Mr. Carlisle has money growing out of his ears. This seems like a big purchase to you, but the man owns more than one island. *Islands,* Olivia. That people live on, and pay him rent. A few pieces of jewelry won't even make a dent in his interests."

"True." Bert took the jewelry and returned it to the box for safekeeping. "But I wouldn't go telling a bunch of people that, Livy. You're bound to create enemies."

"Not to mention getting your jewelry stolen. Okay..." Pat gestured toward the chair. "Let's do hair first. I think half up, so the necklace and earrings are visible, but curly strands falling down like dewdrops. That'll look beautiful."

Pat got to work, her hands moving quickly and efficiently as she went about her task. Bert made up plates of nibbles and passed them out, trying half of each plate in the process. He didn't partake in champagne, as he was driving, but the man could certainly eat.

After hair, we went straight to makeup. "Natural is definitely the way to go. We don't want to overpower the dress or compete with the necklace—Mr. Carlisle could've made great strides in the fashion industry." Pat got to work with the same smooth efficiency she'd employed with my hair.

"Oh wow." Bert moved beside Pat when she had finished, staring down at me. He smiled. "Yep, you look really pretty, Livy. Really, really pretty."

"All I did was enhance things." Pat started putting her items away, leaving a couple of things on the couch that she'd used—probably for later touchups. "When she hits thirty, and the rest of that baby fat melts away, she will be a knockout! She won't need any makeup."

"She doesn't need any now," Bert said with a furrowed brow.

"Yes, she does, Mr. Ramous," Pat countered with a flat voice. "She is twenty. She *looks* twenty. No one takes twenty-year-olds seriously. Give her some edge to those cheekbones, and a pronounced shelf to hang those eyebrows, and she is a twenty-year-old with *distinction.* Society is a fickle bitch—it wants youth in women, but it doesn't want to listen to that youth; it just wants to stare."

Bert gave me a put-upon expression as he shook his head. He had no idea what she was talking about. He was among company.

"I'm twenty-two, by the way," I said, trying to hide a smile.

"Same thing." Pat shooed me toward my room. "Go get into your dress. We are ten minutes behind schedule."

"I can see why Hunter likes to work with you. You're an extension of his pushiness."

As I entered my room, my gaze snagged on the contract lying on my bed. I'd gone over it the night before, page by page and line by line. Most was the same, and most didn't really matter. I was to be his plus one to events, acknowledging that he would provide anything needed to make the role a success—like clothes, accessories, etc. I was to make myself available on nights and weekends if the job demanded it, and other things I was already doing. I hadn't realized this was part of the personal contract—I'd thought it was the requirements of the job, and covered in the contract of employment.

The only issues that remained, the ones I had any problems with, were the sexual ones. He got to call *all* the shots. I had to answer to his beck and call. I couldn't instigate, and had a limit on saying no. My job was on the line for each infraction, not to mention the normal things that could get me fired, like being late, or not doing my work.

There was more, though. I worried that with a contract, Hunter would shut off. He'd get to keep his head in business while he robotically satisfied his physical needs. I couldn't deal with that. Right now he lost control enough to show a softer core when he touched me. He showed his passion. If he had yet another coat of armor protecting him, as this contract would provide, I feared the softer, caring man would disappear. And that would make my role unbearable. I couldn't stand to let that man go.

I adjusted myself within my dress, tucked away my uncertainty over my future in this position, and walked out into the living room. Pat looked up and squinted immediately. "Let's put the jewelry on, because right now, your makeup is too subtle." A smile creased Bert's face and softened his eyes. "Livy, you will knock them dead. They won't know what hit them."

"Yes. Perfect." Pat smiled and adjusted a few strands of hair, blasting me with hairspray, then checked her watch. "A little behind, but we're okay. Let's have another glass of champagne to loosen Livy up, and then we'll check in with Mr. Carlisle."

"I'm not nervous." I adjusted my breasts again, drawing Pat's eyes.

She sucked her lip before saying, "You have a bra on."

Bert's face reddened. He turned away in a jerk, probably to keep himself from looking, and moved toward the table.

"A strapless one, since the dress is strapless."

Pat shook her head. "Take it off. Sweetie, you're twenty. Your breasts are perky and round. They won't be that way forever. You need to let them free while you can. Trust me."

"But…" I cupped the bottoms of my breasts.

"No. C'mon." Pat led me to my bedroom and closed the door. Without consulting me further, she turned me around, unzipped the dress, then unhooked the bra. "You'll thank me for this."

"But…"

She zipped me back up and turned me around. "Much better. More natural. Now your cleavage doesn't look store-bought. You are a masterpiece." She kissed her fingers like an Italian might while admiring a plate of delicious pasta.

"I feel really exposed," I said as I looked at myself in the mirror. "More comfortable, for sure, but… People are going to notice."

"Oh, people will notice you. That is a given. Bert's right—you're going to blow them away. People pay good money to look like you, and I don't mean on hair and makeup."

She slapped my hands away from my chest. "Leave it. C'mon."

I moaned as she led me to the living room.

Bert handed me a glass of champagne as Pat said, "Drink one now, one in the limo, and one on the plane. You'll need it. I get the feeling you don't know what you're walking into."

"What am I walking into?" I asked in confusion.

"He's here!" Panic laced Bert's voice. He dropped his phone into a pocket and came toward me. "Down that, Livy—no, drink it. You'll need it."

"He's early," Pat scoffed.

"Probably thought she might try to run." Bert smiled as he waited for me to gulp my drink down before ushering me toward the door.

"Shoes!" I said.

"Where's her wrap?" Pat asked, zooming around the room, picking things up.

"And the mess!" I glanced back at all the food and wrappers on the table.

A black silk wrap was thrown over my shoulders as Bert bent to my feet with my heels. I put my hand on his huge, meaty shoulder to balance as I lifted my foot.

"I'll just tidy up really quick," Bert said as he slipped on the second shoe.

"You're not coming?" I asked in sudden panic. He'd become my cheerleader, of sorts. He was the guy that thought the same way I did about Hunter and the job—my silent partner in crime.

"Pat and I'll be in a separate car. I'll speed—it'll be fine." Bert straightened up, gave me a once-over to make sure I looked okay, and nodded. "I'll walk you down."

The buzzer rang. Bert put his hand out to keep me put as he pushed the button and said, "Yes?"

"You have an entourage now," Pat said with a bounce in her step as she finished packing all her stuff. "And because you'll enjoy it, I'm going to enjoy it. I love to witness someone's first time."

"It's me," came Hunter's voice through the speaker.

A wash of excitement passed through my body as I heard his voice. And then a pang of regret, knowing that if I didn't sign that contract, I would miss hearing that deep timbre. I'd miss seeing those smoldering eyes in that handsome face. I would no longer get to run my hands along that magnificent body, or be wrapped in his warm embrace.

"We were just bringing her down," Bert said before pushing the other button to open the building door.

"I'm coming up," we heard.

"Wants to check up on me, huh?" Pat said, and sipped her drink. She didn't look worried in the least.

My heart stopped when the door opened, giving me a glance at the man behind it. Hunter wore a tux perfectly molded to his outstanding body. His wide shoulders and strong arms reduced down into a trim waist. Gold cufflinks adorned his sleeves and black shoes shone beneath his tailored pants. He'd shaved and his hair was done in a messy style so popular among celebrities. Those eyes, always hooded, as if he were in the throes of ecstasy, looked me over.

His gaze met mine. He walked forward slowly, fire burning in his eyes. "You are stunning."

I smiled from my toes, falling into that entrancing stare. I stepped forward to meet him, standing close enough to feel his heat. "Thank you," I said in a breathy voice as I looked up into his handsome face.

"You're fifteen minutes early." Pat interrupted our moment in a blasé voice. "We had to make her gulp her champagne."

As if emerging from a fog, Hunter blinked, his eyebrows lowering slowly. He took a step away from me as his gaze turned to Pat. "I wanted to make sure she had everything. This is her first event."

"I think we're ready, sir," Bert said as he gathered up the items he'd brought and replaced the mess on the table.

"I trust you have extra hair products?" Hunter asked, circling me to look at the dress. I caught his gaze shoot past me into my bedroom, and then snag on the contract strewn over the bed. To anyone else it was just some paper haphazardly thrown around, but when his brow furrowed and his jaw tightened, it was clear he knew exactly what it was, and he knew I was doing my homework.

When he was standing in front of me again, his look was assessing.

"I have everything she needs, and another two girls to assist should the worst happen, including a bursting dress, though I don't think we'll have a problem. She could've gone a size smaller."

"She's perfect." Hunter moved toward the door. "Shall we?"

I walked out the door, Bert and Pat following me. At the stairs, Hunter said, "Wait."

I stopped as he moved around me, passing within inches of my body. His smell wafted up and tickled my nose, so divine I had to close my eyes and savor it just to make sure I remembered it perfectly. When I opened my eyes again, he was looking at me with his hand held out. "You aren't steady in heels. If you fall, I want to catch you."

Out of the corner of my eye I saw Pat look over at Bert with wide eyes. I didn't have time to analyze it, though. When I took Hunter's hand, electricity surged through my body, making me gasp.

Trembling, trying to keep it together, I let him help me down the stairs. At the bottom, the progression filed out of the building. Hunter, still holding my hand, led me to a black stretch limo waiting in the street.

He handed me in, waiting until I was settled before moving around the car and getting in the other side. Once seated, he raised the divider between the driver and us.

"Sure we have enough space?" I asked nervously as Hunter poured a glass of champagne and handed it to me. He poured himself two fingers of a dark liquid from a crystal decanter.

"Space, privacy, and comfort, yes." Hunter turned to me, his eyes closing the two feet of distance between our bodies. "You are so beautiful, Olivia. I almost want to call this off. I don't want to share you."

I sipped my champagne to hide my delighted smile, but it didn't help the surge of butterflies in my stomach. He could be so sweet when he let himself. He said all the right things, and in such a deep, heartfelt way that I knew he was genuine. It was a shame he felt the need to keep up his defenses all the time. Everyone else missed out on the exceptional man beneath the armor.

"Did you have any questions about the contract?" he asked in a low voice that dripped with intimacy.

"Can I negotiate things like saying no?" I asked seriously, trying to keep my wits about me as his fingers trailed up my arm.

"Would you say no?" he whispered, placing his palm on my shoulder and trailing a thumb up my neck.

I broke out in goosebumps. "I want the option."

"As I said, I need that role to fulfill certain needs. If there comes a point where you no longer want physical intimacy, I need just cause to discuss it with you. The contract provides that."

"You don't need a contract to discuss that with me, Hunter, and you know that."

He leaned forward, pulling me to him. His lips glanced across my shoulder and up the base of my neck. "I want you now."

"And now I would have to say no," I whispered with my eyes closed, feeling his other hand crawl up the inside of my thigh. I widened my legs so he could gain more access. "Because you will mess up hours of preparation."

"That 'no' wouldn't count toward the five."

"But that's the thing." I moaned as his fingers dipped into my panties and slid across my sudden wetness. "You're making the rules."

"I'm not as rigid as you think." His fingers started up a fast pace, boiling my blood as pleasure pulsed in waves. "I want you as mine, Olivia. I want your signature as a promise of that."

"What about me initiating? I have needs, too, and I don't have time to go out and try to find a guy. I'm always at work."

"I don't want you finding someone else," he growled, his fingers working faster. I moaned, clutching his shoulder.

"I have needs," I whispered.

"I'll meet your needs. I can amend that in the contract, as long as we set strict rules regarding when."

"I'm not worried about you saying no—you don't seem to have any problem with that." My breathing sped up.

"I am."

The limo pulled to a stop. Hunter swore under his breath. "Are you close?"

His thumb rubbed the top of my slit as his fingers worked inside, trying to get me to climax before we had to get out. Pleasure was rising. The heat was taking over. But no, I wasn't close. Not with all the distraction of knowing that someone was about to open the door.

"No," I panted, pushing his hand away. Barely a second after Hunter pulled away, the door opened, allowing a gust of chilled air to flash-freeze the sweat on my face. Hunter rolled out the other side, issuing a command that had the driver backing away from the car.

I checked myself over, adjusted the necklace, and let the fervor recede, before climbing out of the car. My sex pounded, on the rise pleasure-wise, and now I wondered what had gone wrong that I couldn't finish. I took a deep breath outside the limo, willing the tightness in my body to relax.

"I apologize about that," Hunter said into my ear as I glanced at our surroundings. "I wasn't thinking."

I gasped as I looked up at a plane that didn't say Primmer & Locke as I'd expected. It only had one name scrawled along the side. Carlisle.

"You have your own jet?" I asked incredulously as

Hunter ushered me toward the door.

"Doesn't everyone?" Pat asked from behind us. I hadn't even noticed her walking up. Bert's vehicle was parked beside the limo. He was helping out two girls from the back.

"I don't like using the company transportation. It's usually less than adequate, and the approval system is arduous."

The inside of the jet was white leather adorned with stylistic ornaments. On each headrest lay a red strip of fabric with an emblem embroidered into it.

"What is this?" I asked, running my fingers on the gold crest.

"It's my family crest."

"Is this your family jet?" I sank into a plush leather seat in the middle of the jet.

Hunter sat in the chair across from me with a small table between us.

"No. What funds my father intended to give me have already been imparted," Hunter said with a harsh voice. He looked out the window. "We have no more ties other than blood. No more shared holdings or mutual interests."

If I didn't know any better, I would swear pain was working through his words. His eyes, too, had a tightness around them that hinted at anger, but also hurt. He was struggling with something. I was no stranger to feeling hostility toward a parent, but this was more than that. His father must've caused him a great deal of hurt for

Hunter to not only shut down, but to express his emotion plainly before he did.

Fascinated, I stared, wanting to ask more about it. Wanting to see if I could open him up and get him to trust me with whatever burden he carried. People were gathered around us, though, and the plane gave a soft shudder as it began to roll forward. Now wasn't the time.

Chapter 14

WHEN WE ARRIVED, we stalled beside the limo. Pat touched up my hair and makeup as Hunter checked in with Brenda in the office. Eventually he turned to me with his arm out. "Ready?"

"Ready for battle, huh?" I asked quietly as we made our way through the parking lot toward a grassy area. The afternoon was old, throwing long shadows across the ground.

"Always. And remember, you'll be under fire. Some of the women will try to get information out of you, though of what sort, I'm not sure. I don't pretend to know what goes on in the minds of women."

"Understatement."

Hunter steered me to a path that cut through the grass. "Some of the men, though, might see if you can be swayed to work for them. People will assume you are exceptional for me to have chosen you. I advise you to politely decline and walk away. Some of them are great salesmen."

"And don't have personal contracts."

Hunter's jaw tightened but he didn't respond.

A large tent stood in the middle of the grassy area. From within, voices floated out on the breeze, a soft murmur punctuated by occasional laughter. Round tables dotted a wood floor, with flowers and candles acting as centerpieces. At the front of the tent was a bare area where a microphone stood. Behind it several men and women in suits and dresses played string instruments.

Heads turned as we entered. The noise level got distinctly lower.

"Mr. Carlisle, glad you could make it!" A man in his fifties stepped forward with a hand outstretched.

"Mr. Smith." Hunter shook the man's hand with a straight face. "This is Olivia Jonston."

"Hello, Miss Jonston," the man said, putting out his hand for me. "Lovely to have you."

"Thank you," I said, shaking his hand.

"Let me show you to your table." The man walked forward, leading the way with a hand outstretched. "I trust the journey wasn't too long?"

"It was fine," Hunter answered.

"Great, great. And will you be staying in the city, or..."

"We'll be heading back tonight."

"Yes, of course." The man stopped in front of a table near the microphone. "Please, let me know if you need anything at all."

Hunter ignored him as he took the wrap from my shoulders and draped it across one of the chairs. "Do you want to leave your clutch here?" he asked. "It'll be safe."

"With a makeup team standing by, I hardly need it for my lip gloss." I put my clutch on the seat. When I straightened, I felt Hunter's hand slide across my lower back until it curved around my side.

"Afraid I'll get stolen?" I asked in a murmur as a man and woman approached.

"It wouldn't be the first time, and it wouldn't be for business. It would be the first time I cared, though."

"Hunter!" A man in his late forties stopped in front of us with a smile. "Good to see you. You remember Betty, my wife."

"Yes, of course. And this is Olivia. Olivia, this is Pascal, one of the big players in the marketing industry." Hunter glanced around, his face perfectly straight.

"I just *love* your dress!" Betty raved.

"Oh, thank you." I smoothed my hands down my front as a man with trays of champagne drifted by.

"Champagne?" Hunter asked me.

"Yes, please."

Hunter grabbed one of the glasses before saying to the waiter, "I'd like a scotch, neat."

"Of course, sir." The man hastened away.

"So where did you two find each other?" Betty asked.

"Why don't you girls go chat while I talk to Hunter about a few things. Once you girls start to talk, we're suddenly all in one big sewing circle."

I stared at him, incredulous. That was an extremely demeaning and dickish thing to say. And the laughter he followed it up with grated.

I felt Hunter's arm tighten, pulling me closer to his body. Apparently he thought so, too.

"C'mon, Olivia," Betty said, seemingly unconcerned by her husband's comment.

"Don't be long," Hunter said in my ear softly as he took his hand from around me.

"So how did you land the most eligible bachelor in the universe?" Betty asked as she walked us away.

Immediately, a woman joined us, dressed to the nines, hair teased and tousled to within an inch of its life, and sporting that heavy makeup Pat had initially wanted to put on me. "Betty, who is this?"

"Olivia," I said, sticking out my hand.

The woman barely touched her palm to mine before looking over my shoulder. Her eyes sparkled with desire. I knew exactly who she was looking at.

"This is Yasmine," Betty said.

"How did you get hooked up with Hunter Carlisle?" Yasmine asked in a sultry purr. The sparkle turned to condensation as she looked down my body, her gaze lingering for a long time on my necklace.

"I work for him, actually," I said. "I'm fairly new, but he generally brings his admins to events."

"Yes, he does. I've never even seen him and Blaire in public together," Betty said in a tone that implied scandal.

"No, he never brings her out. She goes to a lot of events, but she always says he's working. And now we know with whom." Yasmine pursed her lips as she eyed me again.

"I've really only just started." I needed to get out of this conversation. One of the women was fishing for information, and the other was trying to put me on the carving block. I didn't like the motives of either. "Do you know where the restroom is?"

"Trying to get away so soon?" Yasmine smirked and glanced at Betty. "I saw Mary come in not long ago. I'm going to go say hi. Nice to meet you, Olivia."

Yasmine wandered away with a slow saunter. Betty smiled at me. "Don't mind her. She's been after Hunter Carlisle for years. Had to settle for a rich investment banker who doesn't give her the time of day. It appears daddy wasn't as well off as he pretended." Betty's brow rose with wide eyes, an expression that said she was giving me juicy gossip. Or maybe she was implying I should pity Yasmine? I actually wasn't sure.

"Ah. Mhm." I bobbed my head. "Sorry, the restroom?"

"Oh sure. Here, I'll walk you. There's someone that way I want to talk to anyway."

We crossed the open area with the microphone. Betty nodded and said hi to a few people as we passed. I noticed more than a few stares following my progress. The men's eyes usually gleamed, dipping to my chest and no doubt lower as I passed. The women's looks were either suspicious or curious. I paid attention to those that didn't glance my way at all. Those were probably the people I wanted to talk to.

Betty dropped me off near the restroom with entreaties to track her down again so we could continue chatting. I smiled and nodded politely, almost bowling someone over in my haste to get away. I was starting to have second thoughts over the part in the contract about being the plus one.

As I walked back to my table, a woman sidled up and stopped in my way. Tall, slim, and drop-dead gorgeous, she wore a super-tight blue dress that molded to her body and popped out her breasts. Golden hair fell around her model-worthy face in loose curls, and light blue eyes assessed me with a pretty scowl. "So, you're the new admin, huh?"

My brows crawled into my hairline. "I work for Hunter Carlisle, yes…"

"*This* is what he's going for, huh? Bambi-eyed and curvy…" She huffed. "He doesn't much care for brains anymore, I guess. You probably walked in and dropped down to suck his cock right away, huh? Those of us who actually have two brain cells to rub together got overlooked by a pretty face."

"I just interviewed like everyone else…" I said with sweaty palms, blindsided by the venomous hatred and jealousy she was throwing my way.

"Yeah, I'll bet. Well, watch yourself. I've met his fiancée, and she'd feel much more comfortable with me handling his affairs than someone like *you*."

I stepped away, her cold blue eyes following me. I didn't think that conversation warranted a closing statement. She'd said plenty.

Although I kind of wanted to tell her that I looked like crap when I interviewed. There was no way he'd hired me for my looks or taste in clothes, and since I hadn't given in to his advances, it wasn't for that, either.

In other words, all I'd had was brains. *So thank you very much for the compliment on my appearance tonight.*

Happiness shedding from me like glitter, I found Hunter near the table standing with two men. He was looking at me with a faint scowl. When I got close, he stepped toward me and once again put his arm around my back. "Are you okay?"

"Just had an interesting conversation with one of your other applicants…"

"I've never known one of my admins to…have a good time."

I giggled, smiling up at him. With his handsome face, and showering me in affection, he could've been a prince in one of the storybooks. "She basically said I got the job for my face and my suction ability."

Hunter led me away from the table, not bothering to excuse himself from the conversation. We exited the tent into the cool night air. His brow had crumpled into a frown. "And this is amusing you?"

"Yes. Or don't you remember what I looked like when I interviewed?"

He stopped near a large tree, turning to face me. "I do, yes."

"So she delivered a compliment. I've met jerks before—I can easily ignore that part of the...discussion."

His eyes filled with longing as he looked at me. He laid his hand on my neck before stroking my jaw lightly with his thumb.

"Don't people find it strange that you're always with an employee, rather than your fiancée?" I asked in a whisper, feeling the thrill from his contact.

His eyes roamed my face. "I don't care what they find strange."

"Do your admins care?"

"They've never mentioned it if they have. Do you care?"

"I mean..." I shifted, feeling the light breeze. "I've been with you, Hunter. And you're engaged. I didn't think much about it at the time, but it's not right. And always touching me, with your arm around me—that's got to reflect poorly on her. How does she feel?"

Hunter gave a sardonic smile. He let his fingers trail across my shoulders. "She is the most promiscuous woman I've ever met. Her life bores her, so she reaches for sex to cure her of idle time. To continue to find a thrill, she now has to reach for the outlandish. I first learned of her tastes when stumbling upon a three-way in my living room. That was tame compared to what she engages in now. I'm more concerned with her habits reflecting poorly on me."

I grimaced. "Then why are you with her?"

He shook his head in small jerks. "We signed a contract benefiting our fathers, and indirectly, benefiting us so as to be rid of them."

"How long have you been with her?"

He brushed a strand of hair from my face. "Three years. And before you ask, I haven't broken it off with her because I didn't intend to. The contract is complicated and extensive, and it's allowed me to sever ties with my father. Marrying her would fulfill my duty, and after, I would be free to terminate the obligation at any time."

"What about kids? A life? Hunter, that seems pretty dismal."

He lightly traced the bottom of my lip with his thumb. "I'll never have kids, Olivia, and the life I live is fine. There is security in dismal. I know what to expect."

"It's lonely."

"I'm okay with lonely," he whispered.

"Are you sure?"

Uncertainty crossed his face before I saw a deep and profound hurt steal his expression. His eyes almost dripped with it, a pain so acute it pinched my heart with its potency. Before he could answer, someone said, "Well, well, I'd heard a rumor Hunter Carlisle would be here."

Hunter stiffened. His eyes, a moment ago so open and expressive, turned hard. His hand gripped my shoulder in something that seemed both possessive and like a reflex.

A man of about Hunter's height sauntered up with a beautiful girl that looked about my age on his arm. She had fake boobs, a strangely narrow nose, and lips much too big for her face. If I had to guess, this girl had been through a lot of plastic surgery.

It was the man who gave me pause, though. Tall, broad shoulders, and an unmistakable handsomeness that age hadn't withered. He looked strangely familiar.

"Father." Hunter shifted away from me and dropped his hand to his side.

My eyes widened as the man looked me over. "And who is your pretty guest?"

"This is Olivia. She works for me." The distance Hunter put in those words surprised me. I glanced at him, only to see a wary, guarded look I'd never seen before.

"Olivia..." Hunter's father let the name curl into the air like smoke. "Beautiful name to go with an absolutely beautiful girl. I'm Rodge, since I doubt Hunter has spoken of me." He stepped forward with an outstretched hand. I clasped it and was surprised when he glanced his lips off my knuckles. His eyes dripped lust and possession. His lips lingered past what was polite.

"Hi." I ripped my hand away, uncomfortable.

"Aren't you going to introduce your date?" Hunter asked with scorn.

"Of course." Rodge turned to the woman and laid a hand across her shoulder. "This is Cami. She agreed to accompany me tonight."

"What about your wife?"

"She and I don't exactly see eye to eye on Cami." Rodge smiled and threw me a wink as he explained, "She and I haven't seen eye to eye on much lately. Divorces will do that."

I gave the expected smile, since saying "yuck" would be frowned upon, and angled my body toward Hunter. I really wanted to walk away.

"I know why you're here, son," Rodge said in a taunting voice. "And I know how you work. I think charm and experience might win over the prodigy boy sitting on top of his corporate throne, especially since I trained you to be what you are."

Hunter's body went rigid. He stared at his father for a moment with his jaw clenched. Without a word, he turned and started walking.

I hastened to catch up, following him into the tent and to our seats. He didn't say a word until he pulled out my chair. "Sit."

Taken aback by the curt demand, I did, waiting for him to sit a moment later. Around the tent, others were laughing and chatting, finding their way to their seats. Dinner would be up shortly.

"You okay?" I asked quietly as someone took a seat across our table.

"He's going to go after Donnelley. If he gets the deal, we'll most likely have to go through with the merger. Donnelley is the best option for me, and my father knows it."

Donnelley was the head of the company Hunter wanted to take over. "Will it help your father as much as it'll help you?"

Hunter huffed with derision. "No, not at all. He doesn't have the resources to properly harness what Donnelley has to offer. He's doing this as a big fuck you."

Someone came around with salad as the last of our table took their seats. A smiling man walked up to the microphone in front of us. Before I would be overshadowed by everything else, I quickly asked, "And what about your reaction with me? Is it because of your—"

"He always wants what I have," Hunter interrupted, pain mingling with a sneer in his voice. "If he saw my affection for you, you'd be his primary target. He'd love to take another one from me."

"To take—"

"Excuse me." Hunter got up and walked off toward the restroom.

I watched him go with wide eyes. I could take that comment to mean Rodge had taken an admin or two, which would make a lot of sense, but the desolate look in Hunter's eyes meant Rodge had stolen something infinitely more precious.

Hunter might be hiding from love now, but I bet it wasn't always like that. It seemed that being lonely was safer than having his love ripped away.

Chapter 15

"OLIVIA, JUST WAIT here, I want to speak with someone." Hunter left me at the edge of the tent.

Dinner had passed with the woman next to me gabbing, and Hunter speaking to the man next to him. The only words I'd said to him were to ask him to pass the wine. He had barely even looked at me.

I glanced around for my entourage, but they were nowhere to be found. Pat had a habit of springing up out of nowhere and dabbing me, or fixing my hair, or giving me lip gloss, but after that, the woman blended in pretty well, because I never saw her. Her assistants hadn't been needed at all.

I rocked back on my heels and pulled my wrap around me, trying to wait patiently, but bored out of my mind and just wanting to go home. The issues with Hunter were unsettling me.

"He left you alone?" Rodge moved in beside me and gave me a charming smile. "He hasn't left your side all evening, I've heard. That's rare treatment for an admin of his."

"I'm new. He probably thought I'd get lost or something." I gave him a tight smile.

"Hmm. Maybe so. You're a very pretty girl."

"Thank you." I pulled my wrap tighter around me.

"I see he's layered you in jewels and wealth—that's usually my way. Makes you feel even prettier, doesn't it? The fine clothes and people following you around, fixing your hair…"

"It's a nice change for a lazy girl, certainly."

He laughed, low and intimate. His arm brushed mine. "Yes. But he can be a bit harsh, can he not? Hard to swallow at times. I should know, I've been around him all his life."

"Mmm. Mhm."

"All I'm saying is, I know how to treat a woman. I buy her what she likes, *whenever* she likes. I spare no expense when it comes to happiness. And with age comes a great deal of…" His finger traced down my arm. "Experience."

I flinched and scowled up at him, not able to help my reaction. I could only handle so much flirting—touching made my skin crawl. "Having breasts doesn't make me an idiot, Mr. Carlisle. If you knew how to treat a woman, you wouldn't be getting a divorce."

I should've walked away after that. But what he'd said about Hunter galled. It was his *son*, for cripes' sakes. Whatever had gone down between them, Hunter planned to marry someone he didn't respect, or even like, to get away. That said something.

Remembering what Bert had told me in the beginning of my job, I said, "Hunter may be moody, but he's genuine. He shows people their value. He is direct and honest, and someone I trust. What he *isn't* is a guy that dances around with pretty words and lingering kisses while offering to buy them. I don't know what your deal is, but creeping up on me like this sure isn't honest. You have a long way to go to prove you're a better man than Hunter. Now, if you'll excuse me…"

I walked away with my head held high and my gut churning. I had gone *way* overboard to a rich and powerful man. He wouldn't like being talked to like that, and I had no idea what the repercussions might be.

Not that I planned to apologize. He was a first-class jerk. I didn't need his kind creeping up on me.

I was walking toward the parking lot when I heard my name. I glanced back, only to see Hunter coming up with powerful, purposeful strides. I stopped, crossing my arms against the chill.

"I thought I told you to stay put?" Hunter shrugged out of his jacket.

"I don't need—" I rolled my eyes when his jacket draped over my shoulders, then pulled it tighter and reveled in the warmth and Hunter's smell.

"The limo is on its way." Hunter led me to the side, away from the soft glow of the lights illuminating the path, and stopped beneath a large oak tree.

"I was waiting there, but…" I blew out a breath and watched people wandering toward the parking lot. "Your dad walked up."

He didn't speak. I looked up at him, not able to see his eyes in the darkness. "I kind of…wasn't very nice. But he was offering me money, or whatever, and just being kind of gross—I don't know. I wasn't really thinking."

"I heard." Hunter leaned closer and brushed my jaw with his lips.

"What do you mean, you heard?" I closed my eyes, reveling in his touch. "I didn't see you."

"I was walking up behind you when he stepped to your side. Forgive me—I should've stepped in right away. I just…"

"What happened between you and him?"

Hunter placed his hand on the side of my neck gently. His thumb brushed the bottom of my lips as he said in a quiet voice, "There is such an innocence about you. A morality. Right and wrong is ingrained—you don't need contracts and rules. You just need to look inside yourself for guidance. I envy that about you. I find it so refreshing. You are a remarkable woman, Olivia. Your beauty is only one facet of that, and not even the most awe-inspiring."

His thumb stroked over my cheek as he leaned closer. His lips touched my forehead, and then the tip of my nose. I waited, hoping, wanting his lips against mine. Instead, he glanced his cheek off mine and put his arms around me. "I heard you defending me. Thank you."

I slid my palms up his sides, relishing in the hard muscle. "I stole the 'showing' thing. Bert said that when I first met him. It was true, though."

"Bert is a gem, as well. And he likes you a lot. He even came close to chastising me for treating you badly."

"You know his first name?" I said with a laugh as I ran my hands down his back.

His phone vibrated in his pocket. He took it out and read the screen. "Limo is here. C'mon, let's go. I'm eager to get back."

THE RIDE IN the limo with the others was frustrating, because I could see the heat and longing in Hunter's eyes, matching my own. The plane was also frustrating: staring at each other, wanting, but having to keep our distance. Finally, after forever, we made it back to San Francisco.

"Do you want me to take Miss Jonston home, sir?" Bert asked with puffy eyes. He had worked a long day without any relief—he was probably exhausted.

"No, I will. You see to Pat and her assistants." Hunter handed me into the limo and walked around his side.

As the door shut, excitement took over me. My core tingled and my stomach swirled. Hunter sat in and looked to the front of the limo. After the driver climbed in, he picked up the phone, waited for the driver to pick up, and said, "Stop at Miss Jonston's house, but wait there until I get out of the car. We won't be needing you to open her door."

"Yes, sir," I heard from the front of the long vehicle.

The divide went up. Hunter pulled me close, kissing up my neck as his hands reached behind me to undo my zipper. My breasts tumbled out, bouncing. He pushed me back against the seat before fastening his mouth to one of my nipples.

I moaned while running my hands over his large shoulders. His mouth released my nipple with a pop of suction. "Take this off." He gave the dress a small yank.

"Yes, sir," I purred, getting out of the dress and peeling off my panties.

"Mmm," he said, pulling my thighs toward him. My body slid down, my back on the seat and my legs spread in the air. "So beautiful," he murmured as his eyes lingered on my face. His gaze slid down my body before his mouth dipped to my sex. He sucked in my lips before parting me with his tongue. He licked up to the top and sucked in my pleasure center.

"Oh." I rocked my hips up into him, feeling his digits enter me. They plunged hard and fast. His tongue swirled before he sucked, then swirled. Sucked. My body wound up, and my breath became ragged.

"Oh, Hunter. Oh. Oh, Hunter!" I grabbed fistfuls of his hair. Pleasure consumed me, heating me up and pushing me to the edge.

"Hu-Hunter—" An orgasm exploded through me. I shuddered with a cry of ecstasy. I arched, languid after that release.

"I can't wait," he growled, out of breath. "Suck my cock."

"Yes, sir," I said with an excited smile, grabbing for his zipper as he hastened to undo his shirt buttons. I worked out his shaft and slid my mouth along it, tickling his tip with my tongue before sucking it in.

"Oooh, Olivia," he said, stripping off his shirt. He grabbed a handful of my hair and lifted me off him. His lips found my throat while he rose up. I pulled at his pants, getting them and his underwear down to his ankles. He kicked them off.

"I wish we had a bed," Hunter said, coating my hot skin with his touch. "I can't go slow," he breathed, lifting me into his lap. He lined us up. Hands on my shoulders, he pulled me down onto him.

His hard length filled me. I let out a long, loud groan. His palms found my breasts, teasing my nipples. I swung my hips and closed my eyes, soaking in the delicious friction. I bounced, driving down onto his cock.

"Yes, Olivia," Hunter said. He encircled me with his arms before rolling us to the seat. His body landed on top of mine before we spilled to the floor. He thrust, hard. My head craned against the seat. My legs were straight up in the air. His position was equally as awkward, but he didn't slow. He pounded deeper into my hot depths, ripping moans and small screams from my throat.

"Tell me," he panted, his hard chest rubbing against my taut nipples.

"Take me, Hunter," I groaned as the waves of pleasure started to coalesce.

The limo stopped, but Hunter did not. He pumped into me harder, his lips next to mine, his labored breath splashing across my face.

"Oh God," I moaned, clutching his back. My core wound tighter. The pleasure prickled my body pleasantly. "Yes, Hunter. Fuck me." My words got higher and higher. My begging grew louder and wilder. The heat and tingles condensed.

"Come, baby," he said into my ear.

I broke apart, my orgasm ripping through me. Everything shattered, blasted apart. I sucked air into my lungs for another long, low moan as wave after wave of climax thundered through me. He quaked over me, emptying into my body as I squeezed him tight.

We slowed, slick and lying awkwardly, but neither of us moved. I wanted him to stay inside me for a while longer. I craved that comfort that his body could provide.

"Don't leave me, Livy," he whispered into my ear. "I can compromise a little. I can make it work so you're happy."

"I'll think about it, Hunter," I answered honestly, hugging him close.

He sat up and glanced at the floor before helping me to the seat. He helped me get dressed first, securing me with a wrap before throwing on his own clothes. "I'm trusting you with the pill," he said quietly, not looking at me. "I've not done that with anyone else for ten years. Don't make me regret it."

"Please," I finished for him.

"What's that?"

"Nothing. I just help you be polite by finishing your commands for you. And I don't give a crap about you—my life is a mess as it is. There is no way I'm going skip a pill and bring a kid into this world. Not until I feel like an adult. At least some of the time, anyway."

He looked at me for a long moment before running his fingertips down my face softly. "Ready?"

We exited into the cold. He walked me to my door and hesitated once there. Facing me, he brushed my cheek with the back of his hand, longing on his face, his gaze glued to mine. "See you tomorrow."

"Okay," I said softly, wishing he would kiss me. I wondered what happened to him away from other girls. From me.

I walked into my apartment and went to my bedroom immediately, already missing him. I saw the contract lying on my bed, sprawled out with tick marks where I had pondered the various rules. I thought back to the last look he gave me, reminding me of mussed hair, twisted sheets, and entwined bodies.

I didn't want to be good anymore. I didn't want to be rational. I wanted what all the girls wanted—I wanted Hunter Carlisle, the most unavailable man in the city, and not because of his fiancée. Hell, he wasn't even available to her. He was closed off in his high tower, powerful and elite, and hiding himself from the world behind contracts and suits.

I wanted to strip all that down and find the man underneath. I didn't care what it cost me, or how it might hurt. I wanted to know the real Hunter Carlisle, and I would sacrifice my body, and maybe my soul, to do it.

Chapter 16

———❦———

WITH BATED BREATH and nervous sweats, I walked into Hunter's office on Friday, the last day of my employment if I so chose. He hadn't said a word about it to me yesterday. Not even a hint. In fact, he'd acted like normal Hunter, curt and commanding, with eyes for his computer alone.

I crossed the space with his coffee and a folder. I set the coffee on his desk.

I set the folder next to the coffee.

It wasn't until I was halfway out of the room that I heard the rustle of paper. He'd opened the folder, I was sure of it.

My exhale was audible.

The rest of the day he didn't say a word. When I delivered coffee, he didn't look up. When he passed my desk, he didn't acknowledge me. Messages, emails—nothing.

Toward the end of the day I started getting nervous. More nervous, really. What if he didn't want me anymore? What if he'd done some thinking, too, and changed his mind?

Brenda stood and wrapped a scarf around her neck before putting on her jacket. "Another day in paradise finished. See ya Monday?"

"I…don't know. Maybe?" I gave her a lopsided, comical grin, trying to hide the uncertainty.

"Oh right—negotiations." She winked at me. "He'll give you what you want. He wants you to stay on—he wouldn't have spent time training you and trying to find more important work for you to do if he wasn't concerned about it."

"Negotiations?" I squeaked. My face burned.

She smiled knowingly. "You're worth more than he's paying you—you think I don't know? I say get as much as you can. He can afford it. This company tries to lowball you by saying they have great benefits. Well, benefits are good, but show me the money, too, that's what I say. I barter for my life every year at raise time— so don't let him get off easy, and he'll give you what you want."

I breathed a sigh, and then felt completely sheepish by not remembering that money was supposed to be on the table as well. She nodded in a "go get 'em" kind of way before walking toward the elevators.

I tapped my desk. Should I go in to him?

I worked on a spreadsheet for another fifteen minutes before the need to know my fate started eating me alive. I stood in determination as a shape emerged to my right.

I sat back down.

Hunter came around my desk. He held the blue folder. His gaze locked with mine before dropping the folder onto my desk. "I'm headed out. Have Mr. Ramous take you home. He's waiting by the curb."

"Yes, sir," I said in a soft voice.

"See you Monday."

I felt a thrill as he moved away toward the elevator. I laid my hand on the folder. I was, quite possibly, delivering myself into the hands of evil, but there was nothing for it now. I was signed up.

I opened the folder, expecting a copy of the contract. Instead, I stared at the original as the elevator chimed distantly. I picked it out of the folder. A note fluttered down to the surface of my desk. It read,

"I will trust in the guidance of your inner compass. Monday we'll start the discussions about money. Come prepared. —HC."

I smiled down at the note. His compromise was trusting my judgment, and asking me to trust his. No contracts. No rules. Just mutual expectations and fulfilling each other's needs as they arose.

It wasn't perfect, but life never was.

I closed the folder and felt a surge of hope. Hunter Carlisle was letting me in. It was up to me to push the boundaries.

The End

The story continues in the second book:

Now, *Please*

Chapter 1

I WALKED INTO Hunter Carlisle's office on Monday morning as a sexual equal. I was flying by the seat of my pants, not regulated by a personal contract. Hunter was trusting me. More importantly, he had allowed himself to open up just a crack and let me wiggle in. It was a huge milestone in his life and I was grabbing it by the horns and hanging on.

He was sitting at his desk with the soft light of the morning spilling over his broad shoulders. My breath caught in my throat for just a moment before tingling overcame my body.

The man was gorgeous, and I thanked God that he had come to his senses. Otherwise I'd have to start stalking him. I still might, just for the thrill.

"Hey," I said, putting his coffee on the corner of the desk just as I had every working day for the last month. He glanced up at my voice. His hooded, smoldering eyes reminding me of twisted sheets and writhing bodies. I gulped, a little too loudly. "Uh, I have some things to go over concerning my salary…when you're ready."

He glanced at the clock at the top of his desk before leaning back. "You know my schedule—when do I have time?"

"Now, or at the end of the day. That's pretty much it."

Hunter clasped his hands in his lap as he studied me. His gaze slid down my body before nodding. "I have other plans for you this evening. Sit."

My stomach flip-flopped. The expectation of what he had planned gave me a hot flash. I sat gingerly and tried to ignore the pounding in my core. I handed over my folder.

Hunter took it without a word, opened it, and glanced at the contents. He laid the folder on his desk. "I know what kind of work you do, Olivia. What kind of figures do you have in mind?"

I took a deep breath. I'd thought pretty hard about this. Realistically, I was getting paid six figures to do a job worth half that, while having sex with the hottest man alive. I would do the last for free, so really, I was way overpaid.

I couldn't very well tell Hunter that, though. He was a business prodigy the CEO of a huge, global company without even seeing thirty candles. He expected me to shoot high, and then barter hard.

I leaned forward and opened my mouth to spout out a ridiculous number when the phone rang. Hunter glanced at the display, then ripped the handset off the base. "Yes?"

I slowly closed my mouth and leaned back. The man could ignore a grenade blast if he had business to attend to.

"When is this?" Hunter asked with a sharp edge to his voice. He listened for a moment, checked his watch, and then clenched his jaw. "Who else will be there?" After another moment, he finished, "Get me booked in. Rearrange my schedule and move any meetings I can't miss to online. I need to be there."

He was about to put the phone back in the cradle when he paused. His eyes flicked to me. "Yes, she's going."

He set the phone down. "Negotiations will have to wait. The board has given me a limited time to secure a takeover. If I fail, which they hope I will, we'll go ahead with a merger. Donnelley—the owner and CEO of the prospective company…"

He waited for my nod before continuing, "He's attending a business summit at a resort in Nevada. This means he's shopping around for a buyer. He knows what his company is worth—or, more frankly, what its tech rights are worth—and he's ready to offload. He can't handle the size the company has grown to, so he's ready to cash out."

"Well…that's great, huh?" I asked, trying desperately to care. My brain was still lost on what he had planned for later that night.

"Yes, but he doesn't like me. He won't want to sell to me if there's any way of avoiding it."

"Are there other companies willing to offer him as much as you?"

"A few." Hunter swiveled in his chair so he could gaze out the window. "My father's company, for one."

Intense loathing colored Hunter's voice. Saying he and his father didn't get along was putting it mildly. His dad was the root of Hunter's current distrust of others, distance from intimacy, and desire to be alone.

I was dying to know what had happened, but Hunter was an isolated, closed-off man. Getting at his depths would need the Jaws of Life.

I settled back in my chair. "If you don't get this takover, what's so bad about the merger?"

"A significant number of layoffs, organizational restructuring, which will drain our budget, and two leaders with vastly different long-term goals. I'll have to force my competition out, which will distract me from leading this company."

My eyebrows rose. "Then why does the board want a merger?"

Hunter shifted and looked back toward his computer. "Short-term gain, mostly. They estimate an increase in stocks, we'll have a larger market share, more reach—there are a great many reasons to do it, but an equal number of reasons not to. If we can get the takeover, on the other hand, we'll have more potential down the road. Most don't believe me, but I know I'm right. They're keeping me on a very short leash."

He faced me again and edged closer to his desk. "My father has a certain type of charm—he can manipulate people like no one else I've ever known. It's him I am competing against for this. He'll play the small business card—he'll say he built his company from scratch and knows the value of company loyalty. He'll talk about it like it's his child. He'll even say he wished his only son would've gone into business with him so he would have someone to pass his legacy on to. It's all crap, of course. But Donnelley will buy it, because my father will sell it. What I need is someone who *really* speaks Donnelley's language. Someone who is starting that uphill climb and trying to figure it out. Someone that loves her jeans and hoodies, just like Donnelley does…"

I raised my hand in the air and then dramatically pointed at myself. "I assume you mean *moi*?"

"Yes, you, Olivia," Hunter said. "You are my secret weapon. You're my charm. I need you to get me in. If he falls in love with you, and sees your loyalty to me, then hopefully he'll warm up to me."

"I don't know about falls in love with." I crinkled my nose.

Hunter's eyes sparkled. The edges of his lips tweaked, as close to a smile as he usually came. "We'll settle for deep respect, then." A stern expression crossed his face—his business mask. "We leave Wednesday, early. Plan for four days, maybe five. Pack some dresses—not too showy—and a large selection of casual clothes."

"Wednesday?" I gasped. I thought over the things I would have to do before leaving. Like laundry, and coffee with Kimberly, and… My mind went blank

Oh, that's right. I had no life.

"Okey-dokey, Wednesday it is." I bobbed my head.

"Use the rest of today to help Brenda get everything organized, learn what you can about Donnelley, and get prepared. You can take tomorrow off to get your personal things ready."

"Oh." I stood, glancing at the folder sitting open on his desk. "Okay."

"We'll talk money when we get back. If you land this, you'll have quite a bartering chip on your hands."

"I don't think bosses are supposed to tell subordinates how to get more money. It's not really in your budget's best interest…"

"I don't think subordinates are supposed to alert bosses when the bosses made a snafu regarding employee bartering…"

"Hmm. Right you are. Forget I said anything." I hopped up and turned to leave.

"And Olivia…"

I glanced back at Hunter expectantly.

"Check in before you leave."

Like a shock wave, a thrill arrested me. "Okay," I said in a breathy voice.

He turned back to his computer as I walked away stiffly. Once at my desk, I took a moment to gather myself. I couldn't wait to see what he was like when he could be completely in charge. When he didn't have to hold back for fear I'd pack up and leave.

With a shaking hand I reached for my mouse. Images of his naked body ran through my head, muscular and delicious. I closed my eyes as I remembered the feeling of him moving inside of me. It had been nearly three weeks. Much too long. I was going through withdrawals.

"Olivia—"

"Ah!" I jumped.

Brenda stared at me from her desk with her lips half turned up in a grin. "What's up with you?"

"You surprised me!" I clutched at my chest as my heart clattered against my ribs.

"I surprised you? I've been sitting here the whole time."

"Sorry." I looked harder at my computer. "I was thinking."

"What were you daydreaming about?"

"Your silence."

"Must've been juicy, whatever it was. Your face is giving you away…" Her grin turned evil. "It's a man, isn't it?"

I leaned toward my computer, staring hard at my email. There was no way I was admitting that I was slipping into dangerous waters with the boss. She'd just tell me all the reasons why it was a terrible idea. Like he was emotionally comatose and I'd get my heart ripped out. Or maybe that he had an arranged marriage set up, and even if he liked me, he was about to marry someone else. Just little things like that.

"Anyway, I'm working on the plans for that retreat," Brenda said. "Do you know what your role will be?"

"Wear jeans, act like a blue-collar worker, and get some business guy to like Hunter. Hunter apparently doesn't care that I'm mostly antisocial. Of all the people he chose to put his faith in…"

"I don't think he knows anyone else who wears jeans." She smirked. "It'll be fine. Mr. Carlisle hates to smile. He hates small talk. Compared to him, you're charming enough to be a politician."

"Is that supposed to be a compliment?"

Brenda's fingers flew across her keyboard. "Could be."

I scowled at her. That didn't sound promising.

"Anyway," she said, "I hope you can pull this guy out of the older Mr. Carlisle's back pocket—that guy gives me the creeps."

"Tell me about it. He all but asked me to be his mistress at that charity dinner."

Brenda's look was scathing. "Disgusting. He's old enough to be your father."

"And rich, which is all some women see. The girl with him was about my age."

"He wasn't with his wife?"

"He said they were getting a divorce."

Brenda tsked. "Typical. She probably grew too old for him. That's his third—no, wait." Brenda glanced at the ceiling, thinking. "The first was Mr. Carlisle's mother, then the maid, then…was there another one before this one?" She drummed the desk. "Yes, this must be his third. He was married to the maid for a while— just to put it in Mr. Carlisle's face, I'd wager. And he calls himself a father."

"To put it in Hunter's face?"

Brenda glanced at me. Wariness crossed her features. She glanced toward Hunter's opened door. Her voice lowered to a whisper. "I don't know much about it. Everything I heard comes from gossip, and *that* came from Mr. Carlisle senior, I think. Hunter has never said a word."

Brenda got up and moved closer, her coffee cup in hand. She glanced at the door to Hunter's office again. "Apparently—and again, this is hearsay—Hunter was in love with the maid. This was when he was young, maybe ten years ago. A little clichéd, I know." She rolled her eyes. "The word is that Hunter loved the maid, his dad found out, and then started having an affair with her himself. Well, she tried to leverage that connection somehow. It got ugly, from what I heard. Hunter's mother found out and threw a fit. She told all of their friends, all of Mr. Carlisle senior's work associates—you name it. I think Hunter was pretty sheltered as a kid— not many friends, not around many girls—so she was kind of it. And then she goes and betrays him… With his *dad*, of all people…"

She quirked her eyebrow and straightened up a little. Her lips pursed. "Damaging to a young guy. To his ego…"

"Yikes." I grimaced, but mostly for show. While that would definitely suck, and certainly be an ego crusher, it didn't smack me as reason enough for a life of cold business and solitude. It was a little weak on the "life trauma" Richter scale. There had to be more.

"You're telling me!" Brenda said, giving me a look before wandering back to her desk. "He's a good guy when you look past the rich-guy mentality. He just needs a hardheaded girl to break him out of his shell."

I snorted. "Good luck. He holds on to his rude *I know everything* act with both hands."

"That's a man for you." Brenda sat back down at her desk. "Do you need to go shopping at lunch, or are you going to take care of that tomorrow?"

"Shopping? Jeans and hoodies was my daily uniform before this job. I miss those days. Now I have to look around for a napkin when my hands are dirty."

"What does a napkin have to do with wearing jeans and a hoodie?"

"My jeans *were* my napkin. That's why they are so awesome—very versatile."

"Gross." I heard Brenda chuckling before the chorus of ticking announced her typing. "I'm ordering in lunch, then. Mr. Carlisle needs to give us a treat for working so hard."

"I'm all for free things."

"Aren't we all."

THE DAY PASSED in a blur of facts, figures, and strange habits about a man I had never met. I felt like a private eye hired for a con. When Brenda shrugged into her jacket, I leaned back and rubbed my eyes. It was half past seven—late for her to be heading home.

"I thought you didn't do overtime?" I asked as she grabbed her purse.

"Usually, no. I don't want Mr. Carlisle to get accustomed to my being here all the time. But at crunch times, I put in the hours and take a half-day when the excitement wears off."

"Excitement, huh?" I smirked and glanced back at my computer. "I'll be working from home tomorrow, I think. I still have a bunch of things to get through."

Brenda paused on the other side of her desk. "Get ready for the trip first, and do work last. Mr. Carlisle has a bunch of meetings lined up when he gets to the summit that you won't need to attend. You can catch up then."

"So, lounge by the pool by day, and snuggle up to a perfect stranger at night. Sounds…weird."

Brenda barked out laughter. "Welcome to the job, girl. Welcome to the job."

She walked off to the elevators shaking her head. I scanned my spreadsheet one last time, retained nothing, and drooped against my desk. I was spent. As I didn't need a whole day to get ready tomorrow, I might as well call it a night and finish up later.

I pulled up my instant messenger and sent a note off

to Hunter.

Olivia Jonston: *I'm ready to head home…*

A moment later, I received the reply:

Hunter Carlisle: *Come in here. Lock the door behind you.*

"Please," I muttered to finish his sentence. My stomach rolled and my sex tightened up. I glanced toward the elevators, making sure Brenda had gone. Then I smoothed out my clothes.

Oh God. This was it. I was about to waltz in, on command, and do whatever Hunter demanded.

I brushed my hair out of my face and then wiped my forehead of sudden perspiration. Tingles of nervousness worked through my body.

I was excited, yes. And horny as hell, but…I was going to give him the power. I was going to let him dominate me. It was terrifying. Exciting, but also terrifying.

Okay. Here goes.

I rolled my shoulders like a boxer. There was only one way to find out if I was comfortable with this.

I walked toward the office. Rabid butterflies ate away at my stomach. I stepped through the door.

Hunter sat at his desk, focused on his computer like he always was. Nothing in his demeanor had changed. His shoulders were relaxed. His movements were slow, almost lazy. He was completely at ease, utterly in his element. He was behaving as if the contract was in effect, I had no doubt.

I closed the door with a soft click, then turned the lock. Just him and me now.

Me at his mercy.

Made in the USA
San Bernardino, CA
03 May 2016